About the author

Natasha Soobramanien studied English at Hull University and Creative Writing at the University of East Anglia. She contributed two chapters to Luke Williams' debut novel *The Echo Chamber*, winner of the Saltire Society's Scottish First Book of the Year Award 2011. Natasha was born in London, where she now lives.

GENIE
and
PAUL

Natasha
Soobramanien

Myriad Editions

Published in 2012 by

Myriad Editions
59 Lansdowne Place
Brighton BN3 1FL

www.myriadeditions.com

1 3 5 7 9 10 8 6 4 2

A CIP catalogue record for this book is available
from the British Library.

ISBN: 978-1-908434-17-3

Printed on FSC-accredited paper by
CPI Group (UK) Ltd, Croydon, CR0 4YY

For my mother and father

'Apparently, there has been only one prominent event in the history of Mauritius, and that one didn't happen. I refer to the romantic sojourn of Paul and Virginia here.'

– Mark Twain, *Following the Equator*

'All the previous editions have been disfigured by interpolations, and mutilated by numerous omissions and alterations, which have had the effect of reducing it from the rank of a Philosophical Tale, to the level of a mere story for children.'

– Publisher's note for *Paul and Virginia*, by Bernadin de Saint-Pierre, English translation, *c*.1851

'I have seen Europe from Mauritius, now I will see Mauritius from Europe.'

– Bernadin de Saint-Pierre, *Journey to Mauritius*

PROLOGUE

On the afternoon of Saturday 3rd May 2003, twelve-year-old Jeannot Gaspard set out from home on his bike to visit a new friend. He did not tell his mother where he was going. Jeannot's friend lived in a shack at the end of a spit of land on the west coast of Rodrigues – the wilder side of the island – a few kilometres away from the village of La Ferme, where Jeannot lived. The journey took longer than it might have done: the destruction caused by Cyclone Kalunde which had brushed past the island two months previously was still being cleared, parts of the road impassable due to reconstruction work, and, once Jeannot had turned off onto a track down to the beach, much of it was blocked by fallen trees. When he arrived at what he guessed was his friend's shack, his friend was not there.

Jeannot's visit was prompted by a conversation he'd overheard between his mother and uncle. Jeannot had come to warn his friend, and to ask him some questions. He waited, but his friend did not appear. The following day, Jeannot returned to the shack and again waited, without luck. Having noted on his first visit the exact state of disarray in which a heap of blankets had been left, Jeannot concluded that his friend had not slept there for two nights. When, on Monday (Jeannot having skipped school), there was still no sign of him, Jeannot finally allowed himself to investigate the contents of the small cardboard suitcase left in a corner of the shack, seeking some possible clue to his friend's fate or whereabouts. The unlocked suitcase, on which was painted

3

in pink pearly nail polish a girlishly curly 'G.L.', contained, along with a bundle of clothing, the following items of interest:

- a washbag containing various men's toilet articles, including a razor, a jumbo tub of chewable vitamin C tablets which felt half-full when shaken, plus, rather excitingly, some condoms;

- a passport bearing a photo of his friend with a shaved head, looking some five years younger, giving his date of birth as 9th March 1971 and his place of birth as Mauritius;

- a wallet containing a 500-rupee note, a map hand-drawn on the back of a blank betting slip on which was marked a cross and the name 'Maja', and a strip of photos showing two teenage girls pulling stupid faces – the younger one dark-skinned with curly blue-black hair, the older pale, with heavy-looking dark red hair;

- an overwashed T-shirt bearing a faded, screen-printed tropical island in blue silhouette, superimposed over an orange sunset – much like the 'Rodrigues' T-shirts for sale in the tourist shops in Port Mathurin, except on this one was written 'The *something* Band';

- an old-looking edition of *Paul et Virginie* by Bernardin de Saint-Pierre, in poor condition, with pages missing.

Four days later, the owner of these items was found washed up on the shore by Pointe du Diable, several kilometres down the coast from where he had spent the last two weeks of his life. When his suitcase was discovered in the abandoned shack soon afterwards, it contained all the above-mentioned items – except for the book, which Jeannot Gaspard still has in his possession.

GENIE

(i) The Cyclone

On Saturday 8th March 2003, Intense Tropical Cyclone Kalunde peaked to a Category Five in the middle of the Indian Ocean, southeast of the island of Diego Garcia, reaching sustained winds of a hundred and forty miles per hour. At that same time, almost six thousand miles away in the middle of London, twenty-six-year-old part-time postgraduate student in housing studies Genie Lallan was being rushed into hospital.

While Genie lay unconscious in intensive care, Kalunde travelled eastwards, sideswiping Rodrigues – little sister island of Mauritius, which narrowly escaped – wreaking destruction but claiming no lives, before veering southwards four days later towards the colder latitudes of the southern Indian Ocean, and oblivion.

At which point Genie Lallan, still in London and still in hospital, opened her eyes.

This was not the first time Genie had woken up without knowing where she was. Or even the first time she'd woken up in hospital, if being born was a waking-up of sorts. But it was the first time she'd died and come back to life again.

She'd only died technically. You could say the same about her resurrection: Mam took photos of her hooked up to the wires and drips, and some of the fat pipe forcing breath down her throat, a mechanical umbilical cord. Mam took the photos to show Paul, Genie's big brother, who had been with her the night she'd almost died.

Where is he? Genie mumbled, not yet properly awake.

Mam said nothing, only smoothed the hair away from Genie's forehead.

She was discharged and taken back to Mam's. Her room had not changed since she'd left at eighteen. Walls the same colour. A flaky pink like dried calamine lotion – no, like the pink of something else which she could not quite recall, she thought, resurfacing between naps – with picked-off scabs where there had once been posters. Hazy from medication, Genie turned her attention to a picture on the wall by her bed. A plate taken from an old book. *Paul et Virginie*. A book with engravings she'd liked so much as a kid, she'd surreptitiously bent back the spine to precipitate its gradual falling apart so she could release that picture. '*Le Passage du torrent*'. Against a background of black mountains, a muscular youth stripped to the waist, trousers rolled up to his knees, was standing on a rock in the middle of a swollen river, poised to continue his treacherous crossing. A girl, about the same age, on his back, clinging to him, arms around his neck, had her face half buried in his hair. On the riverbank were banana trees whose broad serrated leaves flapped in the wind – the same wind which was whipping the river into a frenzy of white froth; the same wind which had unfurled the girl's hair from the scarf she had used to tie it back. The girl looked afraid but the boy, smiling up at her, looked happy to be carrying this load, which seemed to give him the strength to carry on.

Genie studied its cross-hatchings minutely for the rest of the afternoon, in between sleep, until Mam entered with a tray. When she drew the curtains, the sunlight was sharp and watery.

There's been a cyclone, Mam said. She had rung the home where Grandmère lived for her regular update and they'd

8

told her. Mauritius was fine, they said, but Rodrigues was devastated. Absolutely devastated.

Genie squeezed lemon into her bowl of chicken noodle soup. Its velvety steam swabbed her nostrils. *Devastated*, she thought. *Shellshocked. Crying. In bits.* She asked again about Paul. Where was he?

Mam shrugged. Are you going to eat that soup or just blow on it?

On her bed were the same sheets she'd had as a child. Deep-sea divers in old-style diving bells waded heavily through a faded violet sea, parting weeds to find chests spilling treasure. When Genie had first started her periods, she'd bled on them and the stains had looked like rusted coins. She hadn't seen these sheets in a while, she realised, as she manoeuvred herself out of bed. It was the same bed she'd always had. She had little strength to negotiate its sagging and felt tempted to let herself be swallowed up in its peaks and troughs. Being back at home was a bit like that. But she was here only temporarily. She couldn't imagine how it must feel for Paul, who had no foreseeable way of finding anywhere else to live. After his last eviction he had told her that he was done with squatting, that he no longer had the energy to make himself anew. A quote from something, Genie supposed, palm against the wall as she struggled to her feet. Weak as she was, she had to go to his room; she had to see for herself.

Genie knew as soon as she pushed open his door, as soon as she saw how he'd left his room. How he had *left*: drawers pulled from their sockets, gutted; shelves cleared in one swipe – all of it gone, even the stupid photos of her and Eloise he'd stuck into a corner of the wardrobe mirror. Just the basics. 'Prison possessions', he called them. He was not lying low at all. He'd gone.

9

Genie opened the wardrobe; sunlight slithered the length of the mirror and fingered the wire hangers inside. They'd been picked clean.

Mam appeared in the doorway.

I couldn't tell you while you were in hospital.

No, said Genie, I guess you couldn't. Where is he?

But Mam said nothing, only walked to the wardrobe door and clicked it shut. Her reflection looked into Genie's and Genie understood.

He never came to the hospital, did he?

No. His things were gone when I came home from my shift in the morning.

He'd taken Mam's suitcase. The one they'd come to London with. But Mam told Genie not to worry, he would surely be back soon. If only because he'd run out of money.

(ii) 1981–82

Genie was five and Paul ten when Mam took them to live in London. They had never travelled on a plane before. They flew for hours over an empty grey desert. When Genie asked if this was London, Paul laughed.

You idiot. That's the wing of the plane.

Some hours later, the captain announced their imminent landing.

That's London, said Paul, sounding almost awestruck, forgetting for a moment how angry he was to be leaving Mauritius. His cheek was pressed to Genie's at the window as the plane banked steeply. He pointed out the sticky webs of light below. Looks like God's been gobbing.

Mam would normally have snapped at him for that *malpropte*, but she seemed not to be aware of anything around her. When the plane began to buck and shudder in anticipation of its landing, Mam seemed equally apprehensive, leaning further back into her seat, hands gripping the armrests, as though trying to resist the inevitable descent.

They were going to live with Mam's family – Grandpère and Grandmère and Tonton Daniel. Genie and Paul had never met them before. They were leaving behind Genie's dad, and Genie's half-brother Jean-Marie, neither of whom had ever been to London. They were leaving behind Mauritius, the only place Genie and Paul had ever known.

Everything they brought with them had fitted in Mam's suitcase. She kept it on top of the wardrobe in her new room.

Mam's was a gloomy room with only a narrow window, the curtains always half-drawn. It had been Grandpère's until they arrived and it was still cluttered with his things: the back issues of *Titbits* magazine; the Teasmaid on the bedside table which Grandmère and Tonton Daniel had bought him for his birthday but which, to their knowledge, he had never used (No wonder, Paul had said, earning himself a slap around the ear, he only drinks rum and he never has to get up for work); the boxes and bottles of old medicines which crowded the ugly putty-coloured mantelpiece; and a stack of old books. Paul would spend hours absorbed in *Titbits*, but if he was feeling restless he would flick through Grandpère's *Teach Yourself English*, reading aloud.

Hello, Mrs Baker. Is Susan there? (Paul's voice posh and mincing, with a heavy Mauritian accent.) Yes, Roger. Please come in. Susan! Roger is here to see you! Would you like a cup of tea, Roger? Yes, please, Mrs Baker, you old bag. You have a very nice home. But you stink of shit.

Or, if he was in a good mood and wanted to please Genie, he would adopt the voices of characters from the TV programme *Bagpuss*, which she loved. But again, some trace of Creole inflected his imitations of Professor Yaffle or the mouse organ mice, rendering his impressions satirical despite his sincere intentions. In return, to console Paul who seemed to miss Mauritius so much, Genie would 'read' aloud to him from Mam's old copy of *Paul et Virginie*, making up stories around the beautiful engravings. And, since it was the book for which the two of them had been named, Genie would cast them both in the title roles. I can't swim, said Genie, so you are carrying me across the river. We are running away from home. And my hair is very lovely.

There was Mam's dressing table, too, crowded with things that Genie liked to look at, particularly the framed photo of Mam with Genie's dad Serge outside their old house in

Mauritius. Genie would marvel at the difference in their looks: Mam's more various, the Indian skin, the Chinese bones, the Creole eyes and mouth, while Papa – Serge – was so dark-skinned that you could barely make out his features. Papa was hard to see in the photo in the way that he was getting harder and harder for Genie to see in her head. There were so many new things – new people – around her. Genie looked like Papa and Paul like Mam but also different – his hair and his skin and his eyes that same colour, but with maybe more of a glow. Like honey, Mam would say, almost proudly.

Once Genie asked where the photo of Paul's dad was.

You can't take photos of a ghost, Paul said.

Is he dead, then? Genie was impressed.

He is to me.

They lived in three rooms on the ground floor and basement of 40 St George's Avenue, a narrow Victorian terraced house in Tufnell Park. The flat was not self-contained: to walk from one room to another involved stepping out into the corridor used by the other residents. Genie was shy of these strangers in their home, but Paul would try to engage them all in conversation – the young *angle* in the squirrel-coloured duffel coat who lived right at the top, or the old Chinese man (*bonom sinwa*, Grandmère called him). But these men seemed as timid as Genie was.

Genie and Paul's play was shaped by the movements of the other members of their household: while Daniel was at poly or Grandmère was in the kitchen they would play in the front room, where the four of them slept; if Mam was at work they played in hers. And sometimes, if Grandpère was out, they would go down to the kitchen to watch television, or out into the garden. But Grandpère rarely went out. He sat at home all day in his chair in the kitchen, where he also slept, watching the horse-racing or the news and drinking

13

rum. Grandpère, they thought, was gradually flaking away. His skin was grey-brown, dusty with a light white scurf like the bloom on old chocolate. Seeing him sober made him as foreign to Genie and Paul as hearing him speak in English. When he stood up he had the grand proportions of a monument, but when he walked he staggered like a man caught in a gale. The unpredictability of his movements frightened them.

So they spent a lot of time in that draughty hallway where once they had played in a garden in Mauritius. They would crunch into dust the dead leaves that had drifted in through the door, or play post office with the pile of mail for ex-tenants who had left no forwarding address. The hallway smelt of damp newspapers, the muddied doormat and the cold air from outside, spiked with the smell of Grandmère's cooking drifting up from the kitchen.

Every morning, when the sun rose to a point where it set the orange walls on fire, Genie would leave the sofabed she shared with Grandmère and Paul and cross the prickly carpet to climb in with Daniel. They would lie there staring up at the ceiling as though contemplating the night sky and her heart would rise like a balloon. They had long, aimless conversations: she would ask him how thunderstorms happened, or why a chair was called a chair or what colour Paul's dad was. Daniel would try to answer but Paul would shout, from the other side of the room, Because it *looks* like a chair.

Or, Don't you talk about my dad.

Genie was sure for a long time that Daniel was Jesus with his long hair, his odd beauty (a different configuration from Mam's: Chinese bones, Creole skin, Indian eyes – green eyes) and the righteous anger never directed at her but often used to protect her. In that way, Paul was like Daniel. As she and

14

Daniel lay there, she stroked his smooth brown skin and tugged lightly at the hairs in his armpits, which were tough and silky like the fibres from the corn cobs Grandmère would strip and boil for them. She asked him if he would ever get married.

Oh, I don't think so, he said. Maybe when I'm ninety.

She would have preferred him to say Never, but ninety seemed quite far away.

How old are you now? she asked.

Twenty-two. It takes a long time to count from twenty-two to ninety.

And then Genie offered to marry Daniel and he cordially accepted. Paul laughed nastily. He chucked aside his pillow and ran across the room, now barred with sunlight. He kicked Daniel's bed and called Daniel a pervert. That was how it usually ended: with Paul getting angry and calling Daniel names. And then Daniel would say something like, Shut up, you little shit. And then Paul would go running to Mam's room next door saying, Mam! Daniel said shut up you little shit. Then they would hear Mam sigh and rise heavily out of bed and come into the room and tell Genie to go down and ask Grandmère to make the porridge.

But Daniel had lied to Genie. Three months after they came to stay, he told them he was getting married.

It was his day off from the poly. He was taking them to the park.

Let's go *popom*, Daniel said, rubbing his hands, Paul screwing up his face at this babyish expression. But still he raced to pull on his shoes. They walked past the knuckly, pollarded elms along St George's Avenue, the pavement wet from recent rain but still crusted here and there with stubborn lumps of dog-shit. Swinging from Daniel's hand, Genie pointed these out to him.

15

How helpful, he said. Thank you, Genie. You have a special doo-dar.

What are you on about? asked Paul.

A dog-do radar: a 'doo-dar'. And then Daniel made a sound like a police siren – *doo-dar! doo-dar!* – which Genie repeated on pointing out further trouble-spots. Paul pulled up the hood of his anorak and, head down, hands deep in pockets, dropped back a few paces, even though he had no friends here to witness his shame.

It was on their way back from the park, after they had stopped off at the sweet shop, that Daniel broke the news. He was to marry a fellow student, Fanchette, in the spring. Strangely, it was Paul who was most upset. It was Paul – barely able to spit out the words around his jawbreaker – who accused Daniel of having lied to them.

A week before the wedding, Genie spotted a clutch of daffodils in a corner of the gloomy front garden, near the bins. It was the first time she had ever seen daffodils. She was shocked by their waxy brightness and pointed them out to Paul. Later that afternoon, while she was being fitted for the bridesmaid's dress Grandmère was making, Genie heard the front door click. She looked out to see Paul in the garden, scavenging for the daffodils. She tried to run after him but Grandmère had her pinned in place.

Res trankil, ta.

She watched as Paul tugged them up, returning with an armful. He went into Mam's room. She heard Mam tell him off.

You should leave beautiful things where you find them, Mam screamed at him. They're all going to die now.

On the day of the wedding, Genie was given a book to carry along with her posy of pink and white silk flowers. It was a small prayer-book bound in white leather with silver-edged pages. Genie thought it as precious and mysterious as a spell-book. She asked Paul to read to her from it.

I am the Resurrection and the Life saith the Lord: he that praiseth my farts, though he were stinky, yet shall I kick him in the arse.

Grandpère did not make it to the ceremony, but was waiting for them at the hall when they arrived for the reception. He swung Genie around and she smelt the chemical smell of the special cream he applied to his flaking skin, which made her think of the kitchen. This was the first time that Genie and Paul had seen him outside it. He had appointed himself barman and was serving drinks at the trestle table in the hall. They took their seats at the top table without him. The tablecloths were decorated with marguerites and asparagus ferns. Mam fussed over them to make sure they were not wilting and, when Genie asked how the flowers had appeared there, Mam told her she had taken them from the garden and sewn them on herself.

Paul tugged at Mam's sleeve.

But Mam, you said you should leave beautiful things where they were, or they would die.

What are you talking about? Mam snapped.

The daffodils! he cried, turning on his heels and running into the crowd of guests.

Shortly afterwards, when Mam was spooning biryani onto Genie's plate at the buffet table, they heard a commotion at the other end of the hall. They saw Paul running away. He had bitten off the head of the bride figurine on the wedding cake. Genie was sent after him. She found him out in the corridor, by the kitchen, where she could hear shouting. Paul was peering through the glass of the kitchen door, and when Genie joined him she saw Grandpère slumped in a chair, long legs splayed out, with Daniel astride him, shouting into his face and gripping Grandpère's wrists to restrain his wildly flailing arms: Grandpère was trying to hit Daniel. Paul turned on his heel and ran to the fire exit, where he pushed down the bar of the door, and left, slamming it shut behind him.

Back at the table, Genie noticed that champagne had been spilt on her little prayer book. The leather cover was buckled and stained and some of the silver had run from the edges of the pages. It was ruined. She put her head into Mam's lap and sobbed. Mam gently pushed her aside, anxious for the silk of her new dress.

From that night on, everything was different. Daniel and Fanchette went to stay in a bedsit they had rented in Islington. Grandpère slept in Daniel's bed. Paul and Genie were supposed to be asleep when Daniel and Fanchette's brother brought him in. They staggered under the dead weight of him, a limp crucifix, and laid him on the bed. There was a businesslike tone to Daniel's voice that Genie had not heard before.

Met li lor so kote, tansyon li vomi liswar. Put him on his side, in case he's sick in the night.

After they left the room, Genie began to cry quietly.

You'd better get used to it, Paul said. She'd had no idea he was still awake. Something in his voice crackled like static. Daniel's going to Canada with her.

Later that night, through Grandpère's snores, Genie heard Paul cry. She slipped her hand into his. He did not push it away.

Some months after the wedding, they went to see Daniel and Fanchette off at the airport. At the Departures gate, Paul barely acknowledged Daniel, turning his back shortly after their goodbye hug. Back home, when Genie asked if he was upset that Daniel had gone, Paul was scornful.

He's the one who should be sad. He's leaving *us.* ⌐
then he said, I hate airports.

The next day, Grandpère came into the front room. He
almost never came into the front room. *Ale vini! Nu pe al
promne!* Come on, you lot! We're going out!

Grandpère had never taken them out before. They trailed
behind him, apprehensive about where he could be taking
them. They crossed Junction Road to Tufnell Park tube
station, descending in the lift and emerging onto the platform
of the tube, which terrified Genie and seemed to her like
being in the belly of a giant hoover.

They got out at Embankment and walked alongside
the Thames, Paul leaning over every now and then to look
down at the water while Grandpère swaggered some way
in front, his long legs incapable of taking smaller steps to
accommodate them. Eventually they saw him stop, and they
caught up with him. Genie thought of Grandpère's skin
when she saw how the bark of the plane trees, which lined
the river, flaked away.

Look, he said. Look at that. Grandpère was pointing to a
great concrete column. Cleopatra's Needle.

He read the plaque aloud in his stiff, heavily accented
English but Genie understood little of what he was saying.
She did not know who Cleopatra was. She did not know
why she had left her needle here. She did not think it
looked much like a needle. Genie looked at Paul but his
face was turned in the opposite direction and she followed
his gaze to a hot-dog stand across the road. Paul stared at it
meaningfully, willing Grandpère to notice, his nose lifted to
the breeze, sniffing it.

They might have been passing en route to somewhere
else but the memory ended there, on the banks of the grey-
brown Thames, the water churned up by the autumn wind,
with Grandpère lurching around, his arms thrown wide,

kuyonad kado, la! What kind of a bloody
nat?

erwards, he went into hospital.

ght Grandpère died, Genie and Paul lay awake in
the dark for a long time. Then Genie felt a fierce little kiss
planted on her cheek. It was more like a bite.

They were not afraid to go into the kitchen and watch
television, after that.

(iii) The Apple Tree

Genie had no memory of the accident, as Mam called it. That part of the night had been edited out so that, when she looked back, it cut straight from her losing Paul in the club to waking up in hospital. Mam said that he must have just left her and run.

But it was not just Paul who was missing. Half of that night had disappeared too. Genie had not been taken into hospital until four am. It couldn't have been later than one am when she'd lost him. What had happened in between? Had she in fact found Paul again? Had they argued? Had she said something to make him leave her?

Over the days that followed, Mam refused to discuss Paul and his 'running away', claiming Genie was too weak and should not upset herself. But if she thought Genie well enough to bring her all the way out here, to her allotment – or *potager*, as Mam called it – well enough to travel out to the fag end of Hackney by bus on a weekday afternoon, to be jostled by shoppers and mothers with buggies and dogged old ladies with trollies, to sit out in the unkind light and the cold and the sour smell of river, surrounded by wasteland and tower blocks, then Genie was certainly well enough to talk about Paul.

Look at my ladies in their Easter bonnets!

They're called daffodils, Mam. Genie was not in the mood for whimsy.

Mam was wearing one of Paul's old T-shirts. A Smiley face in a bandana rippled over her stomach, and it was

21

spotted with tiny holes. Hot from digging, she stopped and leant on her spade. It was the patch where her apple tree had once stood. Mam had lost it in the great storm of '87. She had talked about that tree ever since. She talked about its lost future as someone might speak of a child who had died.

This reminds me of when you were tiny, Mam said. When we were in Mauritius. You used to share a bed with Paul. He hit you in his sleep once and bruised your face. I wouldn't let you play out in the street in case the neighbours thought I had been beating you.

I don't remember any of that.

I made you stay in the garden. You and me in the garden, like this. They didn't like me, those women.

I only remember London.

You were always a Londoner. Not like Paul. He never felt at home here.

A low-flying aeroplane bound for City airport thundered overhead. Genie followed its passage across the white and blinding sky.

I'm worried about him, Mam. Why would he leave me like that unless there was something wrong?

Well, he's not worried about *you*. No word from him since it happened. You could have died. When the hospital rang I was in shock. I couldn't believe you'd done such a stupid thing. As though you'd gone onto the motorway and stood in front of a juggernaut heading straight for you. I went there by taxi. I told myself, If the doctor comes out to see me when I ask for you at reception, she's dead. But they took me straight through. I asked who had brought you in. They said no one. No one, Genie.

Aren't you worried about him?

Of course I am. I have *always* been worried about him. When you have a baby it's not your *baby* lying there in a little blue towelling outfit, you know. It's your heart. The

22

most precious part of you out in the world. Think about when Paul ran away to Mauritius. Wasn't I worried then? And look what happened to Jean-Marie. That could have happened to Paul. I had to stop worrying after that. It was him or me, Genie.

Genie, bundled up in blankets on a deckchair, closed her eyes against the cold March sun. She found herself thinking about apple blossom, the first time she'd ever seen it. Some months after arriving in London, Mam had taken them to the scrubby little park round the corner from Grandmère's. Genie had been shocked to see thick fistfuls of creamy, foamy blossom spilling from the trees. She had felt as though she would explode, as though she didn't know what to do with herself, it was so beautiful and surprising. She had run towards the little stand of trees and Paul followed her, clambering up into one of them. From where she stood, looking up at him, the sky seemed full of the stuff. Paul wrenched off handfuls and scattered the crushed petals over her. Then, seeing how badly she wanted to possess these blossoms, he broke off what seemed like a huge branch and jumped down to hand it to her, he and Mam laughing at her reverential expression.

I want to find him, said Genie.

It's been over a week. Where would you start?

I could try Eloise.

Li pa em kone kot li ete, sanla. She doesn't even know where *she* is, that one.

That was true. The last they'd heard, Eloise had been staying at a rest home for the rich and fatigued. Mam asked about Sol. Weren't he and Paul practically like boyfriend and boyfriend at one time? But Paul hadn't mentioned him for years now. What had happened there?

Genie claimed not to know. She didn't know where he was now.

His best friend! Mam said. How he can just drop people like this.

Maybe Sol dropped him.

Maybe, said Mam. But this sudden disappearing. Just like his dad.

Whoever he is.

Well, I could never have said anything before. It would not have been fair to Paul. He never wanted to know and he didn't want me to talk about it. He thought his father didn't want to know him. That's not true. Paul's father never even knew about him! I tried to explain that. But Paul didn't want to hear.

Tell me, said Genie.

(iv) Mam's Story

Grandmère and Grandpère came to London from Mauritius in 1964, before Independence. They brought Daniel, but I was left behind. I was the same age Paul was when we came to London. I had the right to live in the UK but there was no money for my fare. Grandpère had borrowed the money from his sister to come over. She seemed to think that with this debt she owned our whole family: she worked Grandmère like a slave and even Daniel had to go round to help with chores after school. After that Grandpère refused to borrow more from her. So I stayed with Ma Tante Rose in Bambous and continued my studies. I thought that eventually after I finished school I would get a job, maybe with the Government. I would save the money to join Grandmère and Grandpère and Daniel. But then Independence came and suddenly it was not so easy. I used to have a recurring dream at this time. I was on the dock, waving off the boat that my family were on. It seemed to be moving away, but it didn't seem to get any smaller and it never seemed to reach the horizon. Around this time the Ilois came to live in Mauritius. People from the Chagos Islands. I heard stories of some Ilois who had come to Mauritius in the usual course of their business, but when they tried to go home they were stopped from boarding the boat. Their island had been sold to the Americans. I felt a bit left behind like that too, with my family in England and England no longer having anything to do with Mauritius. It was not just me that was left behind. The whole country was. The mother ship had cut us adrift.

When I left school in 1970, there were no jobs. Mauritians getting jobs in other countries made the front pages of the newspaper. We were always hungry. I remember feeling always a bit faint. A bit dizzy. I got terrible headaches. It was a very depressing time. Very gradually, in a quiet sort of way, we were all starving. It was like we were waiting for something but nobody knew what. There was nothing to do, really. When you went to visit your friends there was nothing new to say, because nobody did anything, nobody went anywhere. Grandpère and Grandmère would send us some money every now and then. But Grandpère was desperate to get his sister off his back so most of his wages went to her. And we never told them how it was for us. We spent our days trying to pass the time. Just for something to do. We patched up our clothes. Went walking in the countryside looking for things to eat. We lived like this for some time. Then one day a friend wrote to me and invited me to visit, she said she had a dress she wanted to give me. So I went to visit her. She was living in Tamarin with her brother and his wife. She was looking after their baby. It was a pathetic little thing that cried all the time. After a while this crying got on my nerves, and so did my friend: there was no dress at all. She had invited me to her house to recruit me for the political party she had just joined – the Mouvement d'Etudiants Mauricien. But mainly she just talked about the man who had founded the party. He was very charismatic, very handsome. He had studied in the UK. He had been inspired by the events in Paris in 1968 to set up the party. I was suspicious of him. I don't know why. Because he was French, I suppose. *En blan.* Because he had brought these foreign ideas to our island when what we needed was to find our own way. I was too listless and my friend's hysteria was draining me. In the end I was sorry I had come all this way to see her. I told her I had to go home and so that I would not have had a wasted journey I asked, before I left, if I could borrow a book. In the bookcase, among the old civil service textbooks in Government English on sugar cane pests, the pamphlets on education, the books of essays by politicians, I found a copy of *Paul et Virginie*. I had read it a long time ago, at school. I had always liked the book. And I liked this edition, which was old. I liked the illustrations. My friend was very scornful. Nostalgic and sentimental bourgeois rubbish which patronises the proletariat and sanctions slavery! Take it, she said. So I set off for the long walk home with the book under my arm. Then I thought to myself that I would go and sit on the beach for a while. We were always warned not to go to the beach alone. The beach could be a dangerous place. Men who have no jobs and do nothing but drink – well, you want to stay out of their way. But I didn't care. I just wanted to be by myself. So I lay on the sands of Tamarin, reading. My friend was quite right about the book. But she neglected to say that it was beautiful, and charming and moving too. As I was reading, a shadow fell across the page and I looked up. It was a white boy. This golden white boy with eyes like light on water. He was carrying a surf board. I had never seen one before. He asked, in English, and in an accent I had never heard before, what I was reading. That's *my* name, he smiled, when I told him. Paul. He had never read the book. As he walked towards the water I stopped reading and watched him. Sometimes staring out to sea can be like looking at a fourth wall if you're on an island: the sea reminds you of how trapped you are. But that afternoon, watching this boy surf, I felt the opposite. I had never seen anyone surf before. It looked so joyful, so free. Like watching a bird on the wind. I stayed for an hour just watching him. When he had finished, he came strolling back up the beach and sat down next to me. The beads of water on his skin caught the sun and made him shimmer. I could hardly bear to look at him. He asked me to tell him the story of *Paul et Virginie*. Then he asked about me. There wasn't so much to say. And what about you? I asked. He came from a place called East London. A place in South Africa! I asked him what it was like. I don't feel at home there, he said. Look at us here on the beach. Where I come from, we'd get arrested for being here together. He scrutinised me. You're so mixed, they wouldn't know how to classify you. And he laughed to himself. Can you believe in my country they classify people! It's worse than slavery, what's going on there. When I looked at him I had the strange feeling that he had holes instead of eyes and that somehow I was looking straight through him, to the sea. That night when I went home, Ma Tante Rose asked if I had a fever. Your eyes look bright, she said. But I felt unnaturally calm, a disturbed sort of calm, as though the eye of a cyclone were passing over me. I said I'd had a good time with my friend. That I would go to visit her again. And so I went to Tamarin the next day, and watched the boy on the beach surfing and spent the afternoon talking to him. This happened a few times. On one of them, he took a chain from his neck and fastened it around mine. It was warm from his skin. The Patron Saint of Hermits, he said. He told me the story of the young man who went to live in the desert. Who was fed by a raven and whose grave was dug by desert lions that guarded his tomb. It was this medal I gave to Paul when he turned sixteen. The one you are wearing now. Soon after he had given me this gift I went to the beach as usual and I sat all day looking out to sea as though waiting for a ship to appear over the horizon. He never showed up and I was left alone there, watching those waves which I had never before thought of as empty.

The day of England's big storm, Genie and Paul stayed at home. They lived with Mam in a place of their own now.

There was no school for Genie, since it was closed. And there was no school for Paul, who had left for good that summer. He had yet to find a job. Together, the three of them watched news footage of people moving in slow motion through flooded streets, of monumental oak trees snapped like toothpicks with something ridiculous and tragic about them, like felled elephants.

Imagine that, but ten times worse, Mam said. That's a cyclone.

Mam told them about the cyclones she'd experienced in Mauritius – how kids would huddle under their parents' beds while outside, roofs and trees and people were just snatched up, whirled in the wind like dead leaves.

Like *The Wizard of Oz*, said Genie.

That's what it felt like when we first came here, Paul said. Like being in a cyclone. Snatched up and then dumped. Emerald City my arse, though. More like pumice stone. Grey, grey, grey, grey, grey, grey.

But Cyclone Carol, Mam continued. *Aiyo zot tu!* That was the worst of them. I must have been six at the time. The cruelty of it was that for three hours, after an elemental battering, we had perfect weather. So people went outside and carried on as normal thinking it was all over but of course that was just the eye of the cyclone. Many of those people died when the eye passed over them.

Crushed or drowned. Yes, sighed Mam, life is more fragile in Mauritius.

Not any more, though, said Paul. They make buildings cyclone-resistant these days.

What do you know? People are still living in shacks in Mauritius.

It's probably all changed, Paul said. You haven't been back in years. Bet there are loads of new buildings there now.

But Mam insisted that if Nature (she often cited Nature where someone religious might have said God) decided to crush you, there was nothing you could do about it. Mam found this out herself when she went to her *potager* two days later and found all her precious plants ripped up as though a vandal had decided to destroy all that was beautiful and good in her garden. Her apple tree torn up from the ground. Nature had destroyed Nature. That was cannibalism, surely, or suicide. And she was crushed.

They were living in a council flat on the eighth floor of a tower block in Hackney. The corridor they lived on made Genie think of a submarine: long and narrow and dimly lit, with an eerie aquatic echo. Grandmère too had moved. They visited her on Sunday afternoons in her new flat to eat hunks of dry cake like mouthfuls of sand. Genie and Paul would twitch with boredom while Mam and Grandmère muttered together, their conversation syncopated by the heavy clock on the mantelpiece.

It was on one such visit, the week after the storm, that Grandmère told Mam she would be buying then selling her council flat under that Government scheme. Her plan was to go back to Mauritius. Her sister, Ma Tante Rose, did not have long left to live. This time, when Grandmère patted her knees and said, *Anfen!* as she usually did to signal the end of the visit, Paul told Genie and Mam he would catch up with them. He wanted to talk to Grandmère alone.

When he came home he told them Grandmère had agreed to his request for a loan to fund a month-long computer course. Mam was delighted, Genie impressed.

The course was in Cambridge. It was residential. But, some days after Paul had left London, Mam and Genie received a letter. The handwriting was familiar, the stamp – in tropical colours – immediately foreign. It was from Mauritius. Genie had never received a letter before. She tore it open.

Dearest Mam and Genie,

I'm not in Cambridge. There was no computer course. I'm in Mauritius.

I never wanted to leave in the first place. Ever since we came to London, I've been yearning to come back. Yes, I know, a funny word. But I can't think of any other way to describe this feeling of something pulling at me – of something missing. London's never been me. You always wondered why I didn't bother with anything, Mam. Why school was such a bunch of arse. Well I've never learnt anything that means as much to me as the names of the streets I'd pretty much forgotten round here in Pointe aux Sables. I'm living in the old place with Jean-Marie. He is showing me my country. We've been everywhere. Me and him and his friends, driving round the island. Yesterday he took me down to Gris Gris on his bike, all the way down south.

I feel more myself here than I've done since I was a kid. I've missed the place. People speaking Creole around me. The fruit on the trees and the dogs in the street. All those mixed-up faces that make so much sense. Don't be angry with me. I'm happy. I'm home.

Home, thought Genie. How could he be, away from me? *How could he?* But she was too shocked to think of this as a question really – to even consider an answer – and so the words hung over her all evening while she tried to finish her homework, while she warmed up her tea in the microwave, while she sat eating in front of the telly, while she carefully washed up her plate and cutlery. When Mam rang, still at work, Genie did not mention the letter. She chatted normally. Finished her homework. Packed her schoolbag. Got into her pyjamas and into bed. Switched off the light. Several hours later, Genie woke to find that she was standing in Paul's room. The bed was made. Without hesitation, she climbed in.

During the long months of Paul's absence, Mam and Genie lived in a state of strange, jaundiced calm. Neither spoke much. Mam's face became pinched from frequent migraines. And it was physically that Genie felt Paul's absence too – a pain in her throat as though she was on the verge of choking, something hard and round stuck in her throat. Genie found it hard to breathe or speak. *The heart is a muscle*, she thought, as she registered the constriction in her chest. Her nights were disturbed. She continued to sleepwalk and in the morning Mam would often find her in Paul's bed. Mam would get agitated then. It's not right, she'd insist, and Genie grew sullen and difficult, feeling as if Mam was pushing Paul further away. They moved sluggishly through an atmosphere that was heavy with Paul's absence, which had now become a presence itself. And then, after almost six months of this, Paul rang.

Yes, said Mam, when the operator asked if she would accept the reverse-charge call.

It was Paul. Jean-Marie was dead. He was coming home. That was all Mam could get out of him. She tried to ring Serge, but his new wife refused to let her speak to him.

He lost his boy, Mam said, helplessly. He lost his boy.

They must be kind to Paul when he came back to them, Mam said to Genie, though she did not look kind as she said it. They should understand that he had experienced something terrible, Mam said, looking terrible. They must not mention this terrible thing unless Paul did. But Mam did not mention the terrible thing *he* had done in leaving them, in claiming a home away from them.

Any sadness Genie felt about Jean-Marie was for Paul. She knew how much Paul loved him, while she herself knew Jean-Marie only from photos now. But during the days after Paul's call Jean-Marie returned to her in dreams: a wicked laugh and hair like hers, a high pair of shoulders onto which the five-year-old Genie had felt herself hoisted. Genie awoke remembering in her body just how it was to be carried like that: like flying and sinking at the same time. These dreams left her light. While thoughts of Paul – the idea of his return – oppressed her, all the more so for her not quite understanding why.

It didn't occur to Genie until she and Mam were at the airport that she might not recognise her own brother. After his flight had landed and the doors parted, knots of people emerged: tanned holidaymakers – couples mostly – and then Mauritians, trolleys heaped with battered suitcases and plastic bags bearing unfamiliar logos. When Genie found herself looking at a young man on his own for a second longer than it took to dismiss him as not being Paul, he met her eyes and then she realised –

Eh – alla lila. Mam nudged her and Genie fell forward, and he folded her in his arms and buried his face in her hair. She wore it longer now.

He looked bigger and more golden than before. He refused help with his bags. On the tube home he sat opposite Genie. She saw how his body had broadened but his face had hollowed out. Then she looked past him to her own reflection distorted in the curve of the tube window, where she had two sets of eyes, as though she were wearing a pair of glasses pushed back on her head. She caught Paul looking at her with a disorientating curiosity – as though *she* were the stranger here – which dissolved into an apologetic smile when she met his glance.

At home, Paul took his bags into his room. Who's been sleeping in my bed? he said. No one replied. Genie and Mam were as shy of Paul as he was of them, it seemed, this young man who'd replaced their skinny, surly Paul.

This Paul had seen death, after all.

He stayed alone in his room until called for dinner. In the kitchen, sitting at the table, Paul seemed too big for the room. He looked as though the flimsy walls could hardly contain him, and if he breathed out too deeply they would fall away. He seemed to know it too: there was something tensed about him, as though he was afraid to take up too much space. Mam barely looked at him as she served the food and joined them at the table.

Genie rolled her eyes. He's probably sick of Mauritian food. You should've done sausages and chips.

He can tell me that himself, Mam said. He is *here*, you know.

But Paul was not listening. More than that, he was silent. Mam and Genie soon realised that his silence was itself a request for silence. They fell quiet and found themselves considering him as he stared at his food, not seeing it at all, inhaling deeply and holding himself still the way some hunting dogs did before swiftly executing an expert act of retrieval in the undergrowth.

That was when Paul told them what had happened in Mauritius, the night Jean-Marie had died. It would not be

34

quite true to say that Paul told them in the same tone he might have used if asking for the salt. But still Genie felt there was something almost casual, something *unfeeling*, in the way he told them.

It had happened the night of Paul's birthday. A whole gang of them had gone out. There'd been a big fight. Paul had gone for one of the gang, Maja. But Maja had had a knife. Jean-Marie had got between them. That was how he'd died. Genie held her breath, not daring to speak. Mam, also quiet, was immobile too: she did nothing to wipe away her tears. But Paul had nothing else to say. He just bent to his plate then and ate as though someone were about to remove his food. He only looked up when he'd finished.

Mo capav gany ankor?

Mam brushed the back of her hand to her cheeks, took his plate and got up to refill it. Genie gaped: Paul, speaking Creole?

Genie asked him about that later on when they went over to the newsagent's to buy ice-cream.

Fabs – they're your favourite, right? said Paul, leaning into the deep-freezer.

Oh, no. I like Mivvis now. Genie was surprised to hear this take the form of an accusation.

They walked outside with their lollies.

In Mauritius, Paul said, lollies come in totally different flavours. Really exotic ones like guava and mango. Even lychee-flavoured.

Genie pulled a face. I hate lychees, they remind me of eyeballs.

Still?

They walked slowly towards the park, licking their lollies in the honeyed light of the late afternoon.

So how come you can speak Creole now?

35

I never forgot it.

Don't they speak English over there?

Yep.

So why didn't you just speak in English?

I wanted to speak Creole.

Creole's like Latin or something. Nobody really speaks it, do they? Well, only people in Mauritius.

Only? There are about a million Mauritians just in Mauritius.

But it's not a proper language, is it? You can't write it or anything.

Actually, you can. It's more fun when you can speak to people in their own language. You feel like you belong.

They sat on the swings. Genie struggled to catch the drips from her lolly while Paul told her about the gang of guys he'd hung out with over in Mauritius – Jean-Marie's friends and cousins. One cool guy called Gaetan.

Genie had a special technique for eating Mivvis: she would suck the juice out of her lolly, then she would bite off the tip and crunch down into the ice-cream centre. There was, Genie felt, a weird parallel between the considered negotiation of her lolly (via her tongue, and the skilful wrist flicks which allowed her to escape rogue drips) and this carefulness she now sensed between herself and Paul. It might have been his new knowledge of death. Death felt like yet another person in Mauritius that Paul knew and Genie didn't. She felt a strange kind of fear and fascination: who were these people? She had always known everyone Paul knew. Not knowing Creole – barely able to remember her own half-brother, whom she would now never know, whom she could not think of as dead since he had only ever really been a memory – and not knowing his friends, not knowing Mauritius, made her feel left out. Genie knew Creole only as the language of adults. The language they were told off in at home.

I would rather be treated like a visitor. Then people would take you out and stuff, and treat you. I would have made them all speak English to me.

Paul nudged her and smiled. *Tilamerd! To tetu kom en burik, twa!*

Just because I can't speak it any more, doesn't mean I can't understand, she said.

So what did I just say?

Something about me being a little shit, she said, trying to detach her tongue from the burning ice.

Yeah, a stubborn little shit. And if you could speak Creole you could answer me back, couldn't you?

It felt like hard work to Genie, Paul's teasing.

Later, he came into her room. She was sitting on the floor, surrounded by her novelty soaps.

Are you still collecting those things?

What does it look like?

Sorry.

She had been collecting them for some years now. All her efforts at self-control, forbidding herself the pleasure of using these soaps (this thwarted pleasure an odd pleasure in itself), all efforts to preserve the integrity of her collection had proved pointless: having been lumped together in the same basket all these years, they had pretty much come to smell of one another.

Paul sat down heavily on the bed.

So, how have you been? While I've been away?

I made some new friends. You don't know them.

Mam told me.

One remaining pleasure the soap collection afforded was categorisation: Genie was now arranging them according to smell, or rather, what they were originally supposed to have smelt of (fruit, floral, desserts). She sniffed the one shaped like a big strawberry. It had lost its smell completely. She put it in a pile of its own.

Mam can't stand them.

So I hear. Apparently they're leading you astray. Who are these friends?

Nicky. Debbie. Mam never mentions them by name, though. They're always *tifi angle* or *tifi nwar*. Whenever I say she's being racist she says she's got nothing against English people. Or black people. She just says, Girls like that grow up quicker. She says she doesn't want to see me growing up too quickly. How can I grow up too quickly? I'm growing up as quick as I'm growing up. I mean, I do have to grow up, otherwise I'd be like a spastic or something. Does she want me to be a spastic or something?

You want to watch it. She's thinking about boarding school. She's been talking to Grandmère about paying for it.

If she does that I'll just bloody run away, man.

Aw, c'mon, Genie…

Like you. I'll bloody fucking run away like you ran away.

Genie! Don't give me a hard time, I've had a –

Don't give me a hard time? What do you think I've been having since you went to Mauritius? It's been horrible without you. I had this pain in my heart all the time. Like you were dead! I wish you *were* dead. I wish – I hope – I HOPE YOU GET HEART CANCER!

And then Genie threw at Paul, with all her might and in no particular order, all her precious, sun-faded soaps.

That evening, Paul gave them the presents he had brought, as if he had come back from just another holiday. A tape for Genie, and for Mam a paper bag full of seeds.

What kind of seeds are these? she asked.

They're a surprise, he said. Plant them and see what comes up.

38

Nothing illegal, I hope. It is a council allotment, you know.

What sort of music is this? Genie asked, looking doubtfully at the cover of the tape. *Seggae*? What's that?

A cross between reggae and *sega* – the Mauritian music at Daniel's wedding.

Genie would only ever play the tape a couple of times. The rhythms were unfamiliar and she couldn't understand the lyrics. Furthermore, to hear this band she'd never heard of, singing in a language she'd heard only with family, disturbed her. And then the tape got absorbed into Paul's collection, which he took with him when he moved in with Eloise two years later, and Genie never saw it again.

As for the seeds, they never took root.

(vi) Bel Gazou

Eloise's mother answered the door in her dressing-gown, its sleeves like the limp wings of some tropical butterfly. She did not seem to recognise Genie, who announced herself as Eloise's friend from school. Eloise's mother looked blank, and then without a change in expression said, Oh, Paul's sister. She might have said more but she was distracted by the cat, a blue Persian with knotted fur, that was stalking past her, towards the open door. Bel Gazou! she scolded, bending to scoop it up, one hand pulling at the gap in her gown, briefly exposing the dark vein which ran across the top of her breasts. Her nails were painted a dull glittery green. You know you are not allowed outside, she murmured into the cat's head. It mewed in complaint and struggled free. Mrs Hayne nudged the cat inside with her bare foot and turned away into the house. Genie took this as an invitation to follow her.

The drawing room had been redecorated since Genie had last seen it. The walls were now dark and glossy, like holly leaves. Eloise's mother sat down and gestured for Genie to do the same. Genie complimented Bel Gazou on having aged so well. She was told in almost admonishing tones that this was in fact Bel Gazou the second, and when Genie asked if Bel Gazou was in that case the daughter of Bel Gazou the first she was told no, this Bel Gazou had been bought from a breeder, Bel Gazou the first being unable to have kittens.

The vet said she was not one of nature's mothers.

Ah, yes, said Genie, remembering the time she had come to stay with Eloise one summer, when Mrs Hayne was away.

I am not really dressed for visitors.

I won't keep you.

Genie explained that she had rung Eloise several times but received no response. She had left messages at this number too. Eloise's mother blamed the cleaner, a Polish girl who was always deleting messages then not passing them on, apparently. But in any case Eloise was no longer living here. She was in East London now, living in one of her father's properties. She was working for him too. Eloise's mother gave a quick cat-like yawn and asked if she might speak plainly.

If she's not answering I can only assume she doesn't want to speak to you. I wouldn't take that personally: you know how messy things got with Paul, how ill she got, and so on. It's been over a year now. I'm sure she just wants to put all that behind her. And you must remind her so much of him and their time together.

Eloise's mother still dyed her hair that same shade of red, Genie noted, as she followed her to the front door. The same shade Eloise dyed hers. This had always made Genie feel uneasy. As though Eloise's mother was overstating her claim to be just that. It had made Genie uneasy long before she'd even known Eloise was adopted.

Genie had never been to Canary Wharf before. The DLR turned on a section of elevated track and a crop of buildings surged up, all of the same green-grey glass. They looked like the crystalline stalagmites in Superman's secret cave. The company's offices were high up in one of the stalagmites. Genie felt increasingly claustrophobic the closer she got: walking first into the atrium, then up into the lift suite where she was shown into the lift itself, then through a maze of windowless corridors – the whole place artificially lit and climate-controlled – until she was so far removed from the outside world, she could have been underground. But instead, here she was hundreds of feet up in the air. It all looked so – so – professional. Just like Eloise herself, she thought, peering through the internal window of her office, struck by how much she'd changed – the hair, the clothes, the poise. An act of camouflage. What had happened to the half-feral thing she'd been when she was with Paul?

As Genie was shown in, Eloise froze, then smiled ruefully, stretching out across the desk in a kind of horizontal yawn, a gesture of the old Eloise, at odds with the suit and the sleekness.

Genie, angered by this nonchalance, felt unable to look at her and moved to the window. She could almost see clouds below as she looked out, and now Eloise was beside her, telling her that the glass was bomb-proof and that the windows couldn't be opened. She tapped the steel window-frames. Then Genie noticed the fingernails, long and red and glossy. She was almost fooled. But the nails were fake, she noticed. Perhaps, underneath, Eloise's nails were still bitten.

You want to know about Paul, she said.

Yes, said Genie. Tell me.

(vii) Eloise's Story

I saw him about a week ago. He was in a bad way. Maybe that's how he always was. Maybe I was always in such a bad way myself, I never saw it. So let's say he was fine. As fine as he ever was. He wanted money. I went to see him at his hotel and gave it to him. I don't know what he wanted it for. I had a few ideas. But I didn't want to know. I didn't want to know about *him*. How he'd been. He told me anyway. He told me about you. What he'd done to you. He was shaking and crying when he told me. I gave him the money on condition he didn't contact me again. Look at me. I have a new life now. Do you know why I broke it off, in the end? Why, until last week, I'd not seen him in over a year? Let me tell you. We were living back near Old Street, just like in the early days. We never saw you. That was only a few months after Paul had found out about Sol. He wasn't speaking to either of you. It was a strange building, right on City Road but somehow invisible from the street. You walked through an iron door into a narrow overgrown garden and this tall, sooted, spindly building. I don't know what it was originally built for. A grain warehouse or something. There were six floors the size of hangars, several huge rooms on each. Paul and I had a floor to ourselves. Our room overlooked the road but you couldn't hear a thing. It did my head in. Everything about it did my head in. That space. I felt like I was drowning in it. A guy on the floor above us had two pitbulls that would race each other up and down the corridor and around the empty rooms. This constant thundering and

43

thumping. They're densely built dogs. They don't corner easily. And their nails! Shredding my nerves. I spent a lot of time in that room alone. A huge room with bare floorboards and everything we owned dumped in one corner like stuff that someone else had left behind. And me, on our mattress, in the other. Paul was out a lot, dealing or partying or both. I just sat indoors on my own, listening to those fucking dogs, getting iller and iller. It takes energy – courage – to live, and I had none. So I just lay there, really. How did it come to that? This past year I've been wondering. I was a kid when I met your brother. We were so free! Constantly on the move. Paul said something once. Wondering what it did to your mind, your sense of imagination to only ever live in the same type of space. Even a big wedding cake house like yours, he said, if it's all you'll ever know. It's gotta do something to your sense of scale. Perspective. But we lived in warehouses, in big old Victorian pubs, council flats, in semis, disused factories... even a boat. It worked the other way for us. We got lost in all that space. And left something behind every time we moved. People, sometimes. Like Sol. By the time we got to City Road, there was very little left and I couldn't think about changing things. And then something happened... Sometimes Paul brought people back. People I didn't like. I didn't like them for all kinds of reasons and you can guess what they were. But this one guy, Digs, he scared me. And, at the time, I was so listless that I really didn't scare easily. He had these steeply sloped shoulders. They were so sloped his neck practically ran straight into his chest. Paul said he looked like an over-sharpened pencil. There was something about his eyes, too. They were like how an ice lolly goes when you've sucked all the colour out of it. They'd been out all night. They came into the room around midday. I was sitting there reading a magazine. Paul's all excited, tells me he's going to Digs's place, Digs wants to show him something and did I want to come too? He didn't live far, just in a block in Hoxton. I didn't want to go. But I got this funny vibe. I suddenly felt I needed to be there, that my being there would keep Paul safe. A lot of Paul's mates were proper East End. People who'd lived in Hoxton and Shoreditch all their lives, like their parents and grandparents. I used to think he just liked villains – that's what a lot of them were – and I could see why because a lot of them were clever in a raw sort of way, like Paul. But now I'm not so sure. I think it was more the strong sense they had of themselves. Who they were. They all lived in the same place they'd been born in, grew up in the same place where their parents and grandparents had grown up. These guys knew where they were from. Who they were. That really appealed to Paul. But when it came down to it, Paul was not one of them. And there was something a bit... *loose* about Digs. I was loose enough myself to know it when I saw it. So I went with them. Digs takes us to his flat, one in a council block round the back of Hoxton Market. As soon as I walked into that place, I feared for my life. The front room of this tiny council flat crammed with – well, it looked like a herd – of occasional tables, all of them crowded with fancy little figurines: sad clowns, dimpled shepherdesses, pigs in fancy-dress. Totally Pound Shop. Impressive how Digs manoeuvred his way around all that tat without breaking anything, telling us to watch this or that as we made our way to the sofa. The place looked so normal and the two of them so spannered, teeth grinding, these horrible grins when they thought they were smiling – the place reeking of Glade and psychosis. Then Digs says, Amazing, isn't it? And I notice the fish tank. It's on the wall-unit. This huge tank. And in it, one solitary, splendid turquoise fish, like no fish I've ever seen before. Its tail is like an ostrich-feather fan. Almost burlesque. Shimmery blue like one of those huge Brazilian butterflies. So I'm looking at this fish and I think, There's something wrong with it. I couldn't work out what. Then I realised. It was absolutely still. Not patrolling its tank like fish usually do, but just hanging there, suspended in the water, like it was waiting for something to happen. And it was. Something was about to happen. Digs asks us what we think of his fish. Goes up to the tank and makes a kissy face. It's a Siamese Fighting Fish, he says. Then he points to a smaller tank on the shelf above. There's a smaller fish in it. Reddish pink and mottled. It has some kind of skin condition. Its tail and fins look kind of ragged, and dragging, like a kid dressed in grown-ups' clothes. Digs tells us he's got to keep them separate; two males in a tank will fight until there's only one's left. Like nick. He can't even let them see each other. You want to see what happens when you hold a mirror up to 'em. Then he turns to Paul and asks which one he fancies. For the fight. My heart sinks but Paul looks blank. So Digs spells it out. He's gonna make them fight. And he wants Paul to bet on one. Double or quits, he says. If Paul wins, he'll wipe his slate clean. If not, he'll double it. OK, Paul says, I'll take the blue one. Digs says he fancies that one too, so they're gonna have to toss for it. And it's Digs who does the toss, Paul smiling to himself, because he can see by now he's walked straight into this one. Paul loses the toss. He gets the red one. He just shrugs. What else can he do? Looks like a survivor, he says. A fighter. You take the pretty one, then. So Digs takes out a small net and dips it into the smaller tank and tips the red fish into the tank with the blue fish. The second it takes for Paul's fish to right himself is the second it takes for Digs's fish to go at him with all the force he's gathered in his hours and hours of stillness. I see the lunge and I close my eyes and when I open them again a split second later all I can see is flashes of turquoise, flakes of mottled red and ribbons of blood unfurling like fag smoke in the water. A second ago I couldn't look and now I

46

can't look away. I can't look away until the blue fish has ravaged that red fish and there's no more movement in the tank, just a flurry of ripped up scales, the whole thing looking like one of those snowglobes you shake up, except the water's pink like dentists' mouth-rinse. That's when Digs dips his net into the bowl, almost gently, careful to avoid his fish, which is just like it had been before the fight – absolutely still. Digs tips the dead fish onto the carpet. Nudges the thing with his foot. Says to Paul, Flush that… My dad always said there'd be a job for me, a flat for me, if I split up with Paul. I could change my life. Up until that moment I could barely consider it. Just thinking about it made me feel exhausted. Sometimes it's easier to go along with the life you find yourself in than to think about changing it. But that morning something kicked in. I had to get out. The way Paul was going, something bad was going to happen. And we had to pay off Digs. In the end I went crawling to my dad. He told me he'd give me the money if I got shot of Paul. That he'd find me somewhere calm to sort my head out. I was relieved. Like he'd made the decision for me. After that I had to stop caring. That's what I told Paul when he came to visit just after we split. That I'd stopped caring. To his credit, he understood. He said he was relieved. That I was better off without him. He ruffled my hair, kissed me on the forehead, and wished me happiness.

Then I went to see him last week, when he called. It fucked me up a bit, Genie. I hope I never see him again.

It was at boarding school that Genie and Eloise first met. But they might never have become friends at all, if Genie had not taken to sleepwalking. One night, soon after arriving, she was found wandering the wood-panelled corridors where the retired nuns lived, a small ghost in pyjamas. These nuns had not retired from being nuns, but from contact with the school and its pupils. In doing so, Genie felt that they had lost some essential vitality, were moving closer to death – a death, moreover, which they welcomed.

In protest at being sent away to school, Genie refused to talk to the other girls. Instead, she allowed her repulsion and fascination with these sequestered nuns to take the place of friendship. She took to creeping around their wing, spying on them. She would hide in the bushes by the large bay window of their peach-coloured lounge, and watch them peacably waiting for death. She came to know their death clothes, their death stoops, their death smell and the gluey yellow death cast to their eyes; and their breath, when she caught a waft in passing, even held a taste of death. Genie would avert her eyes if she encountered any of these nuns in person, for fear of looking death full in the face. Hadn't Paul done just that in Mauritius? And had this not killed something in him?

After the sleepwalking incident, Genie was moved to a room on the chapel corridor. These were single rooms, intended for older girls, but here the housemistress could keep a closer eye on her. A false sense of quiet was maintained in this part of the school to preserve the sanctity of the chapel. Genie would sometimes catch bits of muted hymn in her sleep or wake to the click of rosary beads as they swung from the hip of a passing nun. It was ghostly and lonely there, until she met Eloise.

One night Genie heard a rap on the fire-hatch above her bed. Before she could answer, the little door was pushed open, and a figure climbed through from the next room, onto her bed, and Genie's legs.

Gerroff, said Genie. You're hurting me.

For such an ethereal-looking being, the girl was heavy.

Sorry.

She sat by Genie's feet. She was holding a small bottle. She unscrewed the lid and waved it under her nose and sniffed it. Genie could feel by her reaction that it stung. She held out the bottle.

Want some?

No.

Genie must have sounded afraid. The girl's eyes narrowed.

How *old* are you?

Thirteen.

Christ. They're putting babies in here.

Genie asked the wraith how old *she* was. Nearly fifteen, she said. In her mouth the 'teen' had the sound of a fork tapped on the rim of a crystal glass.

That small door in the wall connected them, and, though they would knock in warning before climbing through, Eloise always ended up treading on some part of her, or she on Eloise. Eloise was so thin, Genie could feel the bones through the blankets as she swore at her. Life, for Eloise, was full of things to swear at. Genie would sit on her bed as Eloise talked about sex in an offhand manner and sniffed that liquid which made her laugh and cry. She always offered

Genie the bottle and Genie always refused, fascinated. Genie liked to watch her. And Eloise would look at her, moon-eyed, and stroke her skin.

Where are you from? she asked Genie one night.

My mum is from Mauritius. And my dad is too. It's a tiny island in –

I know where it is. That's where my mum's family were from. Though they came back to France before my mum was born.

Maybe our families knew each other! Genie gasped. Maybe we're related!

Maybe, said Eloise. Or maybe my family used to own your family.

One Saturday, Genie followed Eloise through a gap in the hedge of the hockey field, out into an alley and down into town. On that first visit, Genie swaggered the seafront like a sailor on shore-leave, dazzled by the novelty. But when, three weeks later, Paul came to visit, she walked around more slowly, wanting to immerse herself in a place she realised she only half lived in, shut away as she was in the convent for most of the week. How white the place was! How she and Paul stood out. And that gave her a sense of the place being acutely English in a way that somehow felt very foreign. Like Eloise. But not like London at all.

They were on their way to the station so Paul could catch his train home, when Genie saw Eloise. It was the first time she had thought of Eloise as pretty, Genie realised, as she approached. Eloise was pretty in the slight, tattered way certain wildflowers were pretty: long-limbed, slim, a long-stemmed flower. It was the ragged fringe and the pale eyes and maybe also the drifts of cigarette smoke that hung about her. But she had dense, compressed features, almost Slavic, which threw you off somewhat. It took a while for people to work out that she was beautiful, Eloise would later inform her.

She was on her way to Roxy's, she said. Eloise had taken Genie there on that first trip into town. She had bought Genie a fudge sundae and sat smoking menthol cigarettes while Genie tucked in, not daring to look further than her engorged spoon, afraid of the boys slapping and thumping the games machines around them: rough white boys with gelled hair and raw skin who were suddenly leaning towards them, staring at Eloise while she blew smoke-rings and stared back with narrowed eyes.

Now Eloise was looking at Paul that same way. And he in turn looked almost hostile, Genie thought, just like one of those sneering white boys.

See you around, said Eloise, sneering back.

The next day was Sunday. Genie and Eloise had skipped mass. They were alone on Castle Hill and walked around the ruins of Hastings Castle, arm in arm. The sky seemed burdened with cloud. Eloise said, You get witches here, you know.

Genie thought about the part of town they had walked through to get there. Where the shops gave up all pretence of being commercial outfits and resigned themselves to what they really were – the front rooms of slumped houses. In the windows old radios and hoovers, hamster-wheels, dusty cakes, collections of old medals from forgotten wars, displays of Fifties-style satin dresses, some faintly stained, hanging stiffly. It was easy to imagine the place full of witches but they were Mrs Cantrips: dowdy, ageing, fusty-smelling spinster witches with worn-out powers and moulting broomsticks.

You're wrong, said Eloise. There's powerful magic here. Black magic. Hastings is built on ley lines.

Genie knew about those. Paul had explained them to her. She told Eloise about his theory, that tube lines corresponded with other kinds of lines: blood lines, ley lines. All kinds of power lines. And Eloise asked, How come you two are different colours?

Different dads.

They clambered onto the ruins and stood looking down at the town, which lay caught in a cracked shell of cloud below. The fishing boats on the beach looked like tiny Chinese slippers and all the town's movement was stilled at their great height. Even the waves out at sea seemed to break in slow motion.

Why do people say they're scared of heights when what they really mean is that they're scared of falling? Genie asked.

They were balanced on the broken wedge of wall, clutching each other, poised just so – so that if one of them moved, she would fall, and if she fell, the other would fall with her.

They're not afraid of falling, said Eloise. They're afraid of landing. If you carried on falling, it would be OK.

Then, almost to herself, Eloise said, The colour of honey.

By summer they were inseparable. And when Genie was in the infirmary with glandular fever Eloise was in the bed right beside her, recovering from a spell of fainting fits. Sometimes Eloise would undress in front of Genie, daring her to stare. Eloise was so pale she looked as though she had milk for blood. But it was her bra that made Genie sad. Genie did not possess one herself yet but the bras she had seen in the laundry pile were teen bras, pretty things. This was an old woman's bra, stiff with rough lace and heavy-looking, the colour of an Elastoplast bandage. Eloise looked so frail, it seemed to Genie that the bra was holding her up.

In the long, liquid evenings they would hang out of the infirmary window, looking down on the other girls in the gardens, feeling the warm air on their faces. It was hard to sleep at night, in the high soft beds. They decided that they would spend as much of the holidays as they could together.

You could come to my house, said Eloise. You could meet Bel Gazou.

Could I? asked Genie, delighted.

Yes, said Eloise. And you could bring Paul.

During the holidays Genie received a card, a scratchy drawing of a woman with long red hair scraped back from a bony face. She was sitting with one knee drawn up to her chin, staring sullenly with bulging eyes. She looked half-starved.

That's from Eloise, isn't it? Paul said. She thinks it looks like her. That's why she sent it.

Her mum's going away. She's asked me to come and stay.

Watch it. She's trouble.

But he did not say anything to Mam.

Genie could not believe Eloise lived in such luxury – in a whole house, one of those huge white ones with pillars, like a wedding cake. Eloise showed her around in a desultory fashion, kicking at the antique furniture, inviting Genie to trail a hand through the rack of evening dresses in Mrs Hayne's walk-in wardrobe – beaded, sequinned, or of slippery satin – Eloise sneering at it all. Genie kept quiet, trying to remember everything so she could tell Paul afterwards. Bel Gazou could not be coaxed out of the wardrobe, where she lay cowering for most of Genie's visit – in the fur section, to Genie's quiet horror and Eloise's amusement.

Genie was shown the collection of drinks in Mrs Hayne's cocktail cabinet – the spirits which were clear as water until Eloise swilled the bottle and you saw the thick oiliness of the liquid; the shapely bottles of sticky liqueurs which, held to the light, entranced Genie with their jewelled colours. They picked off the sugary crusts that had formed on the open mouth of the bottles and sucked on them.

Taste this one, Eloise commanded, sticking out her finger. On its tip was something crystallised.

Looks like bogies.

Taste it.

With the tip of her tongue she dabbed the tip of Eloise's finger. It was bitter, it was sweet.

Guess which bottle that came from?

When she guessed correctly she was rewarded with a swig – Campari. It looked as though it should have tasted of raspberries but instead it tasted like medicine. Genie passed the bottle back to Eloise, who glugged from it and passed it back to her.

Don't worry, shrugged Eloise as Genie realised with a rush of panic that the bottle was now empty, I'll just tell my mum that she drank it all. She always believes me.

Then she said, Let's ring Paul.

He had been planning to meet up with his friend Sol that night, he told Genie. But he cancelled his plans when he heard the slurring in her voice.

What kind of mess has Schiele Girl got you into? he said, when he arrived an hour later. He told Genie he would tell her off the next morning, when she was hungover, so it would hurt more; she wouldn't remember anything he said to her in this state anyway. Then he helped her to the bathroom and held back her hair while she was sick. The vomit was cherry-coloured. When Genie asked, in between retches, where Eloise was, Paul looked annoyed. Your *friend*, he said, has left me to clean up her mess while she dances about in the living room. The Stone Roses, though, he said more gently, so we'll let her off. He stroked Genie's hair and wiped her face with a damp flannel that smelt of lemons.

Then he carried her up to bed.

She could tell by the light when she woke that it was early in the afternoon. She was alone in Eloise's room. Out in the hallway, she saw a bloody lump on the thick pale carpet. It looked like a half-chewed jelly baby. She picked it up and held it to the light. It was a tiny foetus which lay curled like a blue prawn in its sac. It was Bel Gazou's. A miscarried kitten. Genie followed the thick strings of blood which trailed to the master bedroom. She pushed open the door and that was when she saw them: Eloise, with her hair spread over the pillow, her old lady's lacy bra unclasped, her small breasts and large, rosy nipples exposed, and Paul, lying over her, nothing on but the chain around his neck, the medal now hovering in Eloise's face, as though he was trying to hypnotise her.

(ix) The Meeting

Genie opened her eyes, stunned, as the sun kicked sand in them. She felt as she had done ten days ago on regaining consciousness: that same not knowing for a few seconds where she was, or who she was; and if she felt anything at all it was a sense of being scattered, of waking up after an explosion, bits of her blown up all over the place with her limbs all tangled up – tangled up in someone else's limbs, whoever he was, this boy in the bed beside her. His bed. His flat. Where was she? He was still asleep, his face mashed into the pillow as though he'd fallen from a great height, his arm fixed across her like a crook-lock.

Gradually, she remembered. These last few nights she had spent trawling Paul's old haunts, looking for him, all the while knowing somehow that her search was futile. Hadn't Eloise given him money? Would Paul really stay in London? *Their* London? Genie knew that her search for Paul was not so much born of a belief that she might find him as it was a substitute for that belief.

Her days were spent hungover, going back to the places she'd been the previous night, just in case. All day yesterday she had felt odd, as though she were seeing the world through a yellow filter, and when, in the evening, she had gone to a bar that had once been a local of Paul's (each successive night saw her go further back into Paul's past, it seemed), Genie had fallen in with a crowd who vaguely knew him. They looked too cool and at ease with the world to be friends of his. Customers, she guessed. They'd not seen him for a while, they said, but one of them bought Genie a drink and she ended up staying, feeling grimly committed to the evening, becoming increasingly insular with each drink until finally she fell totally silent, feeling like the time she'd got locked in the porch at one of Paul's squats: alone in the house she'd stepped out into the porch, slammed shut the door behind her and pushed against the front door only to find out that Paul – the last person to leave – had locked her in. And drunk in that bar, surrounded by people but barely aware of them, this was how she'd felt: simultaneously locked in and locked out.

At some point, she'd found herself deciding that if she was to continue looking for Paul – assuming he was still in London – she would have to stop looking so hard, looking so *obvious*. She would have to give herself up to chance and see where that took her. So she'd accepted an invitation from two friends of the people who vaguely knew Paul to go on to another bar, where they had met up with some of the friends' friends, and it was in this spirit of determined randomness that she'd accepted an offer from one of the friends' friends, after the bar had closed, to go back to his place. She had had to gently fight off his half-hearted advances – this man whose connection to her was as dilute as the degree of active constituent in a homeopathic preparation – before they'd crashed down together on his bed, drunk, like fallen trees.

Genie could not remember where in London she was until ten minutes later when she opened the main door of the block where the boy lived, and walked out into a street close to what she soon recognised as Smithfield market. Without having a sense of where she was going – but knowing she was not yet ready to go home – she headed for Farringdon station. The sky was white with racing clouds and her face stung from the whipping it was getting from her hair: one of those strong Thames breezes which reminded her that the river was somehow always just around the corner, even though it could not be seen.

Genie's London was a limited place, she realised now – a tight circle described by home, college and the few places she went at night – while Paul's London was unknown to her. She could only search his old London. The one she'd once shared with him. But that search had turned up nothing. She would have to break free of their London altogether if she wanted to increase her chances of finding him. The logical leads, such as they were, had led nowhere. She would have to trust to fate. And now she would meet fate more than halfway. She would tempt it.

Walking by the market, she passed porters in their bloodied and yellowed white coats, heaving around sides of meat. Big lorries lay panting at the mouths of storage depots and in the gutter she saw the leg of a pig, and its trotter, then further along not quite a pig's head, but its face. Genie wondered if they were all from the same animal. And then there were the spots of blood on the pavement. They looked like bullet holes, scorchmarks. Further along someone had trodden in blood and left a smeared boot-print. As she walked down Farringdon Road she saw office workers, young women in their cheap imitations of designer heels, wobbling slightly as they walked. Genie noticed that there were no really old people here. No kids either. Only 'useful' people. They all wanted to be somebody, she thought, and then she thought of Paul: someone who wanted to be somebody else, or, rather, anyone else but himself. Across the road a tabby cat, striped like a mackerel, stalked the gutter, sniffing at something. It looked out of place here, this domesticated wild thing among all the suits.

At Farringdon, Genie waited on the bridge for the first train to come in. It was eastbound. Without thinking, she took the right-hand set of stairs and jumped on. Then, as it pulled away, she wondered if perhaps she wouldn't be more likely to bump into Paul on a subterranean line instead: the Circle line was too airy, too many of the stations part-open to the world outside with cathedral ceilings and pigeons flapping along the platforms. At Embankment she got out, thinking perhaps she'd change to the Northern line, but on a whim she decided to leave the Underground altogether and walk somewhere instead. She was dragged for a moment by a riptide of tourists towards the Thames entrance, until she pulled herself free and walked out onto Villiers Street, past the rows of hooded homeless mummified in their sleeping bags, heads bent monk-like in the warm morning rain. She tried to get a look at their faces. A man by the park gates was selling umbrellas. He must wake up every day praying for rain.

And all the while, as she turned left into the Strand, past the Gothic hollows of Charing Cross station, past Trafalgar Square and up along Charing Cross Road, past places so familiar she barely saw them any more, these central streets which, unlike the streets at home in Hackney, scarcely felt as though they belonged to her, or if they did, they belonged to all Londoners, streets where all kinds of Londoners came together, past places where memories of Paul through the years were layered one over the other so that here she saw him emerge through the crowds clutching a bag full of paperbacks from a second-hand bookshop to disappear into a side-street, down to Bunjies Folk Cellar, or, there, down tin-pan alley, face pressed to a shop window, looking at the drum-kits and further along, stumbling out of the Astoria, blinking in the too-bright streetlights, fucked and boss-eyed after some night, all of these Pauls oblivious to one another, with Genie catching sight of them one after the other from the corner of her eye as they darted through the crowds, Genie struggling to follow them, she did not realise until she reached it that she had actually had in mind a final destination. The hospital. The hospital where she'd been born. No, not *born* – she was hungover, confused. The hospital where she'd almost *died*. She could not call this, her arrival here, now, an accident. But perhaps it would lead to one; perhaps she would meet Paul here, arriving, too late, to visit her.

Surely, thought Genie, walking slowly around the perimeter of the hospital, when something, someone is so wanted, so that he was almost there in front of her but in some closely aligned parallel universe, utterly unreachable – surely she could, just by wanting him here so badly, will him into existence. Could she not make him materialise in front of her? Summon him like the devil he was?

Passing a side entrance, she observed a group of people smoking with a kind of desperation that made them seem troubled. And they were a group, not simply the relatives of patients or hospital staff on a break gathered casually. They had apparently arranged to meet here. The group seemed to be mainly men in their late twenties to forties, with only a few women, one of them beautifully turned-out, wrapped in a butter-coloured pashmina, whose face, when she turned in Genie's direction, looked deeply ravaged despite the care she had obviously taken with her appearance. The woman was moving to hug a new arrival, her pashmina swinging loose to shroud them both.

When she stood back to readjust it, Genie had a clear view of the man who had just joined them. She cried out then in surprise. At times like this, hungover, Genie had only a fragile sense of who she was, like bad reception on an analogue TV, one of those old black and white ones with the calligraphic aerials: a slight movement, a shift in perspective and she lost the picture. In her shaky state, coincidence was not a rare but meaningless phenomenon. In this state, it felt sinister. This coincidence could mean nothing or everything. She had lost the picture but she had been right after all to stare more closely at the static and find meaning in it. She'd been right all along, she thought, as she ran over to the group, and to Sol.

The Dragon Bar on Leonard Street had been a favourite of Paul's when he'd lived in the squat with Sol on Kingsland Road, but no one ever saw him here these days. The clientele had changed. These people were young, or still knew how to pass as young. Paul had brought Genie here just after her graduation, to celebrate. He'd looked around at these unknown faces and said something odd about wasted talent: about knowing you'd wasted your talent when you turned the bend – when you began to recognise all the places you had passed on your way to whatever point it was that you'd started going backwards. Whatever he'd meant by that. He'd been smoking a lot of weed at the time. And that jacket! It was the one she and Mam had got him for his sixteenth. He'd wanted a leather jacket, the heavy, creaking, rock-god kind, but they'd got him a leatherette bomber from Ridley Road. That was the time Paul had taken to wearing it again. Twenty-six and as skinny as he'd been as a teenager. He'd worn it so often that in the end the leatherette flaked away when he rubbed it, like dead skin. And now she remembered something else he'd said that night. About how lately almost everyone he saw reminded him of someone he'd once known. A lot of things Paul said had been lost at sea. They washed up now and again.

Sol had told Genie he would see her here after his meeting, and, when she felt someone kiss the top of her head and looked up, it was him.

I still can't believe I found you, Genie said.

Were you looking for me?

Well, not quite.

Then you didn't *find* me. You just bumped into me. Nothing unusual about that.

I guess not, said Genie.

They talked about how they'd been. Genie asked about the meetings. He looked better for going, she said. Though she thought he looked as delicate as he always had. Pale and thin. Dark and unshaven. A smudged charcoal sketch of a man.

Two years this month, he said. I had to give all of that up. And how is Paul?

That's why I wanted to meet, Genie said. She told him about the night she'd last seen her brother. Their night out in the club. How she'd ended up in hospital. When Sol pressed for details Genie told him how she'd taken a pill for the first time. How she had nearly drowned from the inside: water intoxication, the hospital had said.

And Paul had been with her that night?

Yes, said Genie, but she'd lost him. They'd heard nothing of him since. He'd run off somewhere.

Sol put his head in his hands. Don't tell me he gave you the pill.

Of course he did. That's why I'm worried about him. It's been three weeks now. I want him to know I'm OK. That I don't blame him.

And then Genie surprised herself by telling Sol something she hadn't even realised she'd been thinking: that maybe Paul's disappearance had been inevitable; maybe it was something he'd been mulling over for a while. Maybe what happened that night had just pushed him over the edge.

That's possible, Sol admitted. I haven't seen him since our big fight. I thought he was running out of options then but, from what I heard from Eloise, things got worse for him. I sometimes think he might have had a different life if he'd never met me.

You can't take the blame. You did meet him at a rave.

No, I didn't. He'd never been to one until he met me. He never told you the real story of how we met, did he? He was too ashamed.

Tell me, said Genie.

(x) Sol's Story

We met in hospital. It was 1990. We were participants on a
medical trial. Don't judge him till you hear what he wanted
the money for. Six weeks, we spent, sleeping next to each
other. He'd told your mum he was off in France grape-
picking or something. I remember the time I first noticed
him. We'd only just started the trial. It was in the early
hours of the morning. I couldn't sleep. I opened my eyes to
find the bloke in the next bed looking at me. His eyes were
open, staring straight into mine, shining like an animal's
in the dark. Then they shut again. Weird. Don't know if
he'd even been properly awake. The next day neither of us
acknowledged the other. It went on like that for a while.
Time's like chewing gum when there's nothing much to do
except be experimented on. There was the pool table, but
that got taken over by the ex-cons and the nutters. The ones
who signed up for the danger money trials. Tests where they
stopped your heart or flooded your lungs or burnt K-holes
into your brain. We kept well clear. We just read or watched
TV. Me and Paul were of a kind. We knew it ourselves. But
neither of us really knew where to start. Then one day, one
of the nurses brings Paul in a backgammon set. He asks if I
want a game. I didn't know how to play. So he taught me.
Not just the rules but the strategies as well. He wanted me
to give him a good game. So we start playing. And, when
we started playing, we didn't stop. We played first thing. We
played while we ate. We played when the doctors were doing
their rounds. We played late at night, using wads of bog roll

to muffle the sound of the dice. When people asked if we weren't bored of playing, we let the clatter of dice speak for us. We played one long game. We agreed that backgammon beat chess hands down for the great swathe of chance that cut across the game play. We liked the speed and the sudden turns of fortune. But, eventually, just playing wasn't enough. Winning wasn't enough. Fear of losing wasn't enough. We began to play for dares. Progressively daring dares. Who would have to give the winner their biscuits at teatime. Who would have to alert the nurse to imaginary side-effects (hallucinations, glow-in-the-dark spunk). Who would have to ask Spider in the end bed if he ever regretted getting that tattoo done. And so we sat there day after day, moving our wooden men across those 2-D spikes, moving them all home. So imagine how we feel one morning when Paul reaches for the set and it's gone. Spider comes up. Asks us if we've lost something. We know it's him but he won't admit it. Then the nurse has a go about us causing trouble. So we give it up. And that's when we started talking. I mean really talking. About ourselves. Why we were in there. Paul wanted the money to go back to Mauritius. He'd gone over two years before, he said. But he'd come running back to London when his brother got killed. Jean-Marie, I remember his name. But there was nothing for him here. He missed the place. Not just Mauritius, I've realised since. I think it was also his brother he was missing – not his brother at all, I know now, but your half-brother. He sounded pretty cool, that guy. Paul told me a lot about him, about the island, about all the things he did over there. But most of all he talked about Jean-Marie. I remember one story about him. Nothing much happened but it made me see him how Paul might have done. Him and all his crew, the ones Paul hung out with, they used to go to this same spot by the river to fish and smoke weed. You couldn't see them from the road.

I remember how Paul described it. The foliage dense and full of litter. They'd sit around, looking out to the processing plants and factories by the docks of Port Louis, and Jean-Marie would say shit like, Call that a capital city? Or, How many Port Louis could you fit into London? I think that's what Paul dug about him. He was bittersweet. Too big for the island. They'd sit passing beers and joints around while they set up the rod over the water, which was smooth with oil. Paul said the first time they took him there, Jean-Marie pointed to this rainbow patch on the water and told him the fish they caught came in its own oil. No need to stick any in the pan when they fried it. And that was what they'd do when they caught the fish – fry it up with garlic and chilli and salt and eat it, hot and fresh, with their hands. So this was how they sometimes spent their Saturdays. But one afternoon, this copper comes along with a sidekick. He's new to the force. He must have seen them on the road and followed them down there. He picks Jean-Marie out as a face and says he wants to search him. None of them can believe this. They're six against two, hidden from the road. And these facts appear to dawn on the man only after he's issued the order, though now he has no choice but to see it through. And he's pretty shitty about it. Probably to mask his fear. Jean-Marie stands up, brushes himself down and raises his arms. Search me if you like, he shrugs. But show me your hands first. Think you're smart, don't you? the cop says, but he still does as Jean-Marie asks. He was probably more relieved than disappointed not to find anything on him. He cut his losses and wisely decided against searching the rest of them. Which was lucky, because Maja was the one who, well, you know – he was holding their *ganja*. Apparently Maja used to like telling Paul, whenever they were smoking, how you could be stuck in prison for possession of just one joint. But this is the bit I love about the story. As the

66

cop turns to leave, Jean-Marie calls out to him in an almost friendly way, I'm going to get you, you know. I don't know when, but I will… I don't know that he ever did.

We got our backgammon set back in the end. Spider was in for eye medicine. Something went wrong. Some kind of discharge. He ended up with his eyes bandaged over. No more pool games for Spider. In the end it was a simple thing for Paul to creep up to his bedside locker and nick back our stolen board. Spider heard him. Sat up in bed, bellowing, waving his arms around like a mummy. Fucking hilarious. We sat by his bed and played our first game in ages, rattling the dice really loudly. This time, when we played, it was different. This time we talked while we played. We talked about music and films. Cricket and football. And girls. And he told me about you. Me, I told him about Berlin – helping to pull down that wall. I told him about squatting. Raving. All the parties I'd been to. The drugs I'd taken. I offered to take him on a night out after the trial was over. To say goodbye, I said. Before you go back to Mauritius. But of course he never went. I think that's where he's gone now, Genie.

(xi) 1991

In the eleven months that Paul and Eloise had been squatting
together, they had moved three times. Now they were living
in an old Victorian terraced house at the Shoreditch end of
Kingsland Road with Sol, among others, and on the night
of her fifteenth birthday Genie came to stay with them.
They were taking her to a club. Genie assumed it would
be a club in the West End; there was nothing round where
they lived. She hated the area, how it was always windy on
Old Street, as if the air itself was in no hurry to linger, with
nothing around but locksmiths, glaziers, sad little sandwich
bars, tatty little offices and pubs with boarded-up windows
boasting live exotic dancers (as opposed to dead ones, Eloise
would sneer). Eloise's name for the area was 'Poland'. But
the club was in Shoreditch Town Hall. And it wasn't really
like a club at all, Paul explained, as they left the house, since
it was one where you could take kids.

As they entered the main room Genie felt as if she'd
walked into a hippie's wedding reception. There were kids
and parents and people of all ages in between or older, those
being the biggest kids: running about in what looked like
clown trousers, batting balloons to and fro and sucking
on lollies, drinking from bottles of pop. Genie had hoped
to get drunk on Southern Comfort and lemonade but no
alcohol was served here. Paul and Eloise didn't seem to
care, though. Genie watched them rubbing up against each
other like cats. Eventually, after noting how Eloise had lost
her spikiness and Paul was not his usual wired self – both

of them becoming something almost molten and fused – Genie guessed they'd taken Ecstasy. She knew they did this regularly but she had never been with them when they had. She felt uncomfortable around these strangers and drifted away.

At the end of the night they came to find her outside in the corridor and brought her back into the hall. Everyone was sitting on the floor. Some kind of weird space-age music was playing. Paul and Eloise found a spot near Sol and pulled her down beside them, just as a huge canopy drifted gently down from the ceiling, trapping everyone together in a benevolent bubble of silk. It was a bit of an obligation, Genie thought, as if you were expected to feel something, but she acted as though she thought it was all magical, the way Paul and Eloise were wanting her to. But Sol gave her a sneaky dig in the ribs and smiled apologetically, even though he too was on a pill.

Afterwards they walked back to the squat. It felt like all the other squats Paul had lived in and decamped from over the past year, the rooms damp and chilly, filled with broken bits of bikes and all kinds of rubbish, lit with hundreds of candles, the windows covered in sheets, the walls in torn patches of old people's wallpaper – large cabbage roses or trellis patterns. It felt at once like home, in that it felt like all the other places they had lived in, but then again not, because they lived in a way that indicated they knew they would have to leave at short notice, like refugees.

Paul and Eloise disappeared while Genie sat in the living room, yawning on the bald velour sofa, the diseased heart of the house transplanted to each place they moved to. She was waiting for them to bring out blankets. She preferred not to enter any room where they were alone, even after knocking. Remembering the time she'd walked in on them could still make her angry for reasons she couldn't fathom. She was jealous, of course, but of what or whom, she couldn't tell. She lay on the sofa and closed her eyes.

Sol, on his way back from the kitchen with a glass of water, asked where she was sleeping. She patted the sofa. There were a few rooms free, he said. The others had gone to some Spiral Tribe thing. She declined. She didn't want to sleep in their beds. They were too relaxed about their personal hygiene. Sol offered her his room. He would take the sofa. If he got her some blankets, she said, she would be fine down here. Suit yourself, he said. Though you could always bunk up with me. Might be comfier. But before she could reply he had gone upstairs. He returned shortly afterwards with a duvet.

Genie woke in the night after a series of dreams filled with flowers. In the first, she had wandered into the school's hockey field at night to find it filled with overgrown delphiniums. They swayed over her. She began to dance with one of the deliphiniums, under a sky whose stars mirrored the many flowers around her. She was naked. In another dream, the large tree outside the school chapel was filled with blossom, and from one of its branches hung a swing on which she sat and rocked. She awoke to hear music coming from the room above. Sol was still awake. She threw aside the duvet and went upstairs.

He lay reading by candlelight, smoking a joint.

Can I stay here? I think I heard a mouse…

Course.

The opportunity to share a bed with Sol thrilled and frightened her. The bed – a mattress on the floor – looked too intimate when Sol flung back a corner of the covers, exposing the sheets. She was embarrassed to look at it. She focused on a pair of shoes instead – proper men's shoes – quite unlike the old school trainers Sol always wore.

Have you got a job interview?

He laughed. His mum had bought them for him. For a wedding. And then she asked if he could put them away because shoes with no feet in them looked spooky to her, like empty eye-sockets. He looked amused and said, Of course, and climbed out of bed. He put the shoes behind a box of records.

Here, he said, passing her a folded T-shirt from a pile. A nightie for you.

The room was dark when she came back from the bathroom. She could smell the affronted smell of a candle that had been snuffed out. She was grateful he couldn't see her, suddenly feeling shy. She made her way round the edge of the room, carrying her pile of clothes, aware of every step. When she slid in next to Sol, she could smell him on the sheets. It was disturbing. She lay awake for a long while, rigid on her side of the bed, anxious not to touch him accidentally, aware that he was not yet asleep either, and that, like her, he was struggling to control his breathing.

Around dawn Genie woke with a lurch: someone had come into the room. The sky outside was light and she could see Paul creeping over to Sol's jeans, cast aside on the floor at the end of the bed. He rifled through the pockets and pulled out a packet of Rizlas. As he turned to leave he noticed Genie. He looked furious.

What the fuck are *you* doing here?

You didn't leave me any blankets.

Go and sleep in Tom or Anke's room.

No. They smell.

Well, let me get you some blankets, then.

Nah. I'm comfy here. What do you think he's going to do? Rape me?

He looked as though he was about to say something. But then he changed his mind and left the room. The noise had disturbed Sol, who shifted and grunted a little in his sleep.

71

Genie leaned close and whispered, Shhh. On a whim, she kissed him lightly on the lips. She did it again, and, without knowing she was going to, slipped her tongue in his mouth. His tongue seemed to melt on hers. He opened his eyes and pulled away sharply.

Woah. Genie...

But she kissed him again. This time, he kissed her in return. She slid her hand under the covers, over his naked chest. Her fingers felt strangely numb – numb in the sense that they were feeling too much – as though their fuses had blown – like that instant of confusion before you worked out if something you were touching was very hot, or very cold. And she discovered what he felt like, which was tense and knotty... smooth and firm and sparsely haired there, and here, feeling him through the thin soft material of his shorts, amorphous, tightening into veins and ridges. She heard the hardening of his breath as she slipped a hand inside his shorts and gripped his cock. His eyes, already closed, closed tighter. And then he was touching her. The more she learnt, she thought, the more she realised how ignorant she was. And when it got too much to look at him she tried to hide herself in his body, burying her face in his armpit, the hollow inside the thin bulge of bicep a rockpool in which she found seaweed hairs and the smell of garden fences warmed in the sun.

He was still asleep but his eyes were not fully shut. She could see a tiny crescent of white beneath the lids, barred by lashes spiked with eye-dew. His eyelashes were long and ragged, like torn netting. She unclasped his arm and got out of bed. Downstairs she made herself a cup of tea and sat watching cartoons, her knees pulled up to her chest under Sol's T-shirt, an intense and unfamiliar ache around her inner thighs.

Paul came in and told her to get dressed.

I'm buying you breakfast. Just you and me.

Goody, yawned Genie. I'm staaaaaaaaarving.

Paul looked horrified. How come you're so hungry?

Genie reminded him that no one else had wanted to eat the night before. I had enough trouble getting a kebab out of you.

In the café, Genie slid her tinned tomato onto Paul's plate.

They make me eat them at school. Every time I look at them I think of the Sacred Heart.

Paul prodded the tragic, pulpy thing with his fork and watched it bleeding weakly.

I never gave you your birthday present.

I thought I had it last night. My night out.

Yes, said Paul, but I've been thinking. There's something else I want to give you. He leaned forward and brought his hands to the back of his neck, unfastening the chain which hung there.

I can't take that.

You can and you will.

He got up from his chair and walked behind her. She felt him brush aside her hair, felt his hands on the nape of her neck as he fastened the chain. It was still warm from his skin.

I don't want you sleeping in Sol's bed again, he said.

When Genie asked why not he said she bloody well knew why not. Please tell me nothing happened.

Nothing happened, Genie said. But so what if it had? She pointed out that Eloise had been fifteen when she'd first got involved with Paul.

Nearer sixteen, said Paul. And Sol's older than I was. But most of all, Genie, you are not Eloise.

On their way back to the squat, they passed through the flower market. Genie stopped to look at a stall full of

73

roses. They were not the ruddy, gaudy kind she remembered from the gardens at school, with the rudely glossy leaves, the blousy bosomy show-roses in pinks and yellow which reminded her of the novelty soaps she used to collect; no, these were antique, puzzled-looking roses, their leaves smaller and darker – almost papery, almost dried. The blooms were strange muted colours, musky, dusky smoky, surly ashen pinks and dusty blues. She tugged at Paul's sleeve. He appeared not to see them. His face was gaunt. For a second he looked made-up: the smudges and hollows, the violet shadows.

You took Ecstasy last night, didn't you? Genie said.

Yep. I've been awake all night. Think I'm still tripping. You get this feeling when it's starting to wear off. It's like the feeling you get when you have a bath. It's almost too much at first, too hot, and then suddenly it's perfect, but that moment when it's just right never lasts long enough. It goes from being too much, to being perfect, to being not hot enough. And once you've noticed it starting to cool off you just know it's only going to get colder and there's nothing you can do and in the end all you can do is get out. Because you have to get out at some point.

(xii) Lost Time

The one place Genie had not yet looked for Paul was the club where she'd lost him in the first place. But she was back here now. Looking for Paul. For her lost hours. Looking for her missing three hours. And now she had found those hours: standing on the balcony, looking down at the dancers, taut and twangy and sharp as piano-wire, the bass like a cathode ray oscillator marking the peaks and troughs of her heart and brain waves oh! and that was when she realised she'd found them, her missing three hours. *This* was where – this was *how* – she'd lost her three hours the night Paul had gone. She had lost those missing three hours being lost! But it was Paul who was really lost. Wasn't it always this way for him? Wasn't he always losing hours here and there on nights like these? Wasn't he always losing nights? And didn't those nights add up over time? How was it to be Paul, wondered Genie, always waking up to feel as if he'd lost something the night before? Would there be a point at which what you'd lost outweighed what you had or what you remembered?

As the numbers thinned out, Genie saw more dance floor than dancers. Mam had always liked to crowd her flowerbeds – she couldn't stand to see patches of earth around the plants. It looked skimpy, she always said. That was what a half-empty dance floor looked like – a skimpily planted flowerbed. Paul had once gone to a club and lost his watch, the one she and Mam had given him for his twenty-first. He'd waited until the end of the night, until the dance floor had cleared, and then searched the floor. Not only had he found his watch, he told Genie later, he had found *many* watches.

The lights came up. The few remaining dancers stood blinking, as though they had just been shaken awake.

Genie found herself in a cab on the way to Sol's place. Minicab drivers were always less interested in where she was going than in where she was from, Genie thought. Their first guess was usually the place where *they* came from. They were usually wrong. And as the driver continued to list possible countries, Genie stared out at the dark streets, absently tracing a finger along the edge of the stains on the back seat, which formed a map of a world, great oceans lapping at the edges of continents.

Then, as they passed along a road she suddenly recognised, she stopped the driver.

I'm from right here.

The house had been repainted since they had lived there as kids, and there were thick, expensive-looking curtains pulled across the windows. The garden had been cleared of shrubs and was now covered in designer gravel, but the old black and white path remained the same, though it was more worn than she remembered it. There in the corner, by the bay window, was where she had seen the daffodils. It was beginning to rain. Soon the rain was flattening the streets in ranks like an invading army. Genie ran until she reached Sol's place, raindrops sliding down her hair, dripping into her face. She rang the bell several times but there was no answer. She had just given up and was walking away when the door opened behind her.

Sol called out, rubbing his eyes.

Genie? What are you doing here? It's late.

She was surprised then to find tears mixing in with the raindrops. As they slid, hot and oily, down her face she remembered how she would always confuse the two verbs in French. *I rain. It cries.*

He looked more closely at her. Christ, you're fucked. It's pouring. Come in. I'll call you a cab.

She'd been looking for Paul, she told him, as he led her down to the kitchen.

As she followed Sol through the hallway and down the stairs, Genie felt uneasy. The shape of the house was at once familiar and not. And now, looking around the kitchen, she realised: this was the mirror image of 40 St George's Avenue. Everything here was on the wrong side. She took in her surroundings: the slick blond floor, the shiny surfaces. She told him that their kitchen had been nothing like this. She told him about the heavy furniture, the grease-stained walls, the divan in the corner where Grandpère had slept. Genie told Sol about the time she'd been left with him, when Mam and Paul had gone to the launderette. Grandpère had switched off the television. The room had fallen quiet. Outside she could see the yard darken. Moss glowed on the dripping walls. Grandpère took up his drumsticks and tapped out a rhythm on the table. *Mu-mee da-dee, mu-mee da-dee.*

I felt really shy. I always did when he spoke to me in English. Then he played again. He handed me his sticks. They were the right size for him – they called him a *longay* (long, high) – but I was a five-year-old kid. I bashed the table. The sticks slipped out of my fingers. Grandpère snatched the sticks up from the floor and shouted at me. He played again. *Mu-mee da-dee, mu-mee da-dee.* He held the sticks so loosely that when he played they looked rubbery in his hands, but when he gave them to me I just held them rigid. Every time he shouted at me I held them tighter. He kept saying, *To pa pe ekut mwa, ta!* You're not listening to me. When Grandpère died, Grandmère said, *Li pa em ena dan li po twi limem*. He didn't even have the courage to kill himself.

Sol was watching Genie drink her tea, like a doctor watching a patient taking medicine. She drank it quickly, so that it burnt then numbed her mouth.

Genie, what are you doing here?

She put down her cup. She took Sol's face in her hands and kissed him. He kissed her back at first in a slightly puzzled way, as though she were saying something he didn't quite understand, then pulled away.

I don't think –

She kissed him again.

Your mouth is hot, he said, whispering into it. And he kissed her back, as if, now, he understood.

She lay looking at him. He opened his eyes and smiled.

You look very white in the moonlight, she said.

Yeah. Horrible. Not like you.

She got off on him being different from her, she said. Angled where she was curved, hard where she was soft. Pale to her dark. She could never have slept with a brown man. It would be like...

She laughed. He stroked her hair.

I think you're right, she said. Paul's in Mauritius. He must be. Eloise says she gave him money. That must have been what he wanted it for.

Maybe he needed it for something else, said Sol. Then he said quickly, He always wanted to go back. Life's too complicated for him here. Don't you ever want to go back?

I don't feel like I was ever really *there*. I remember hardly any of it. No, it's not my country at all. This is.

Then Sol told Genie about his friend, his friend who was always strange: he'd been strange as a child, he was strange at school, he was strange to his family and, even when he grew up and his friends and family had all become used to him, he was still a stranger to them. But then he went to Japan, and in Japan he was not strange. They understood him there. He fell in love with a Japanese girl and married her and never left. Japan had been his home all along and he'd never known until he went there. Then again, Sol said, he knew some people from outside London who lived here and loved the feeling of never feeling quite at home in the city.

I would love to go to Mauritius, said Sol. What's it like?

I can tell you a story about it, if you like. The story of how me and Paul got our names.

Yes, said Sol. Tell me.

(xiii) Paul and Virginie's Story

A long time ago in Mauritius, when the island was still owned by the French, some sixty years or so before the Revolution and a hundred years or so before the British claimed the island, there lived a young boy called Paul and a girl called Virginie. Raised as brother and sister, they fell in love, but, alas, their love was doomed. Dunno if it's a true story or not. It's written as if it's true and something that happens in it – a shipwreck – is true. It's kind of considered half-true in the same way that *Romeo and Juliet* is. You can go to Verona and see Juliet's house and her balcony. So this is what happens. Virginie's mother, pregnant with Virginie, leaves France with her new husband to start a life in Mauritius. Her noble family have rejected her for marrying a commoner so the young couple head out for the colonies where such things don't matter. They want to set up a plantation. The husband travels to Madagascar to buy slaves but while he's there he gets a fever and dies. So Virginie's mum, pregnant and alone apart from her slave Marie, unable to return home now her family has abandoned her, goes to hide herself away in a remote corner of the island. Troubled souls often seek out the wilderness. There's a lot of expressions like that in the book. A lot of stuff about nature and solitude, and how it can soothe us. But in this wilderness she comes across another young woman who has also shunned society. Or rather, society has shunned her. Paul's mother, a simple peasant girl, had been cast aside by a rakish nobleman after she fell pregnant. He never intended marrying her, as he'd promised. So, ashamed, she too has sought out the wilderness and now she lives there, cultivating a piece of land she staked a claim to with the help of her slave, Domingue. The two women become friends and live in adjoining huts, raising their children together, befriended by an old guy who lives nearby. In fact it's this old guy who tells the story. The story begins with someone out walking in the Mauritian wilderness, who comes across the ruins of two small cottages. He wants to know what the story is, so he asks this old guy who happens to be passing by. And the old guy says, I know the story. It's very sad. It concerns two young people and their mothers... so then he pretty much tells the young guy what I've just told you so far. Anyway, this old guy was a hermit, having moved away from society for reasons of his own. He lived near the two women and befriended them. So the little community living in their self-imposed exile was poor but contented, happy to let their lives follow the rhythms of nature. The two slaves married one another and they grew such wonderful things on their plantation! Coconut trees and maize and tobacco and sweet potatoes and coffee and sugar cane and banana trees and cotton and pumpkins and cucumbers and custard apples and mangoes and guavas and runner beans. And the children flourished too. They shared the same crib, their fat little arms entwined, their fat little cheeks pressed together. They bathed in the same pool, drank milk from the breast of the other's mother. If Paul was crying, Virginie was brought over to him to cheer him up. If Virginie was sad, Paul would try his best to make her smile again. Paul became a strong, handsome boy, responsible, brave and loyal, while Genie was beautiful, modest, demure, obedient, soft-hearted and hardworking. The two mothers dreamed of the day when their children would get married, and look after them in their old age. The families were only too happy to live outside a society which had rejected them, but of course they went to church, and on Sundays they did lots of good deeds for those who were less fortunate than they were: visiting the sick, feeding the hungry, clothing the naked and so on. One day, as Virginie was making the family lunch, a runaway slave-girl appeared at the doorway of her cottage. She had been hiding in the forest nearby and was starving. Virginie gave her the food she'd been preparing then volunteered to return with the girl to her cruel master. I will intercede for you, Virginie said. He will forgive you for running away and will not punish you. When Paul returned from chopping wood he escorted the two young girls through the forest, back to the plantation the slave had escaped from. The master, a big ugly white man, was enraged on seeing the slave-girl and was all set to punish her when Virginie interceded. The master took one look at this vision of angelic beauty and suddenly begged for forgiveness, granting it also to his runaway slave. Whereupon Paul and Virginie ran away, into the forest, and headed for home. But they got lost. They wandered for miles, getting cut by brambles, tripping over tree roots and fighting their way through thick undergrowth. They came to a river which was so turbulent, Virginie was afraid to cross it. Paul carried her across on his back, not in the slightest bit afraid to negotiate the slippery rocks, so dedicated was he to the task of keeping Genie safe. They spent the night in the forest, but the next day they were found by Fidèle the family dog, who had accompanied Domingue on his search for the pair. But Virginie was in a state of collapse. Luckily, a band of *marrons*, or runaway slaves, who had witnessed Virginie's kindness to the slave-girl, emerged from the bushes and helped to carry her home. There was much celebration and joy at their return. But after this event things changed. Virginie changed. She became secretive and miserable where once she'd been happy and carefree. Paul's presence, which was once a source of joy to her, now became troubling. Virginie had fallen in love with Paul, it seemed. But her mother considered that she and Paul were too young to marry. And too poor. Marriage would bring children and, with them, greater hardship. Then a solution presented itself. An old aunt of Virginie's mother, bitter and alone but filthy rich, decided that she would make Virginie her heir. But Virginie must come to France to be educated and inducted in the ways of fine French society. Virginie's mother decided to send her to France in the hope of securing for her daughter some of the family money. This was a terrible decision. Virginie was desperately unhappy and homesick, and Paul was filled with unbearable loneliness and rage and jealousy, wondering how Virginie could possibly remain uncorrupted in the metropole, having read about Paris and all the decadence of high society – after a childhood of blissful ignorance, he had begged the old hermit to teach him how to read so that he might learn more about Virginie's new world, but the knowledge only pained him. Finally the old aunt had enough of Virginie, who was clearly pining for her island, her family and Paul, and in a fit of bitterness decided to pack her off back home. But out of spite she insisted on Virginie's travelling straight away, during the cyclone season – a very uncomfortable time to travel by ship, and a dangerous one too. When Virginie's ship weighed anchor just off the coast of Mauritius, Paul was beside himself with joy. But, alas, the ship was caught in a storm and thrown onto the reef. Paul had to watch from the beach, powerless to help, while the ship was wrecked. Domingue and the old man were forced to restrain Paul from throwing himself into the sea to save Virginie, who could be seen on the prow, praying. A sailor insisted she remove her heavy clothes to save herself from drowning, but she refused, out of the unnatural modesty learnt at her expensive convent school. She drowned. Pretty soon after that, they all died of heartbreak – Virginie's mother, Paul, Paul's mother. Even the dog. But not the slaves, for some reason.

(xiv) 8th March 2003

What Genie remembered of that night in the club was this: she remembered settling back into a low-slung sofa feeling as if she were in an airport lounge. She felt prematurely exhausted, as though waiting for a long-haul flight home. Genie was more fed up for its having been her suggestion. She'd asked Paul what he wanted to do for his birthday and he'd suggested they go clubbing. If we're doing that, she'd said, I'm taking a pill with you. He'd been reluctant at first, but she had insisted. They might reconnect, she'd thought. She knew these things were supposed to open you up.

But here she was, feeling very much closed down.

Paul said they were old-school ones, warm, zingy, true – whatever 'true' meant – and like the anxious believer she was Genie had swallowed it whole. Now here she sat with her mouth closed over her teeth because her teeth looked green, she was sure of it. His were – they were flashing as he gnashed on a tired piece of gum, grinning indiscriminately. She told herself it was just the light but it was an insidious kind of light that seemed to have no source. Genie stared up at the ceiling, trying to find it. Paul nudged her, sliding an arm along her shoulder.

You alright?

Yeah, fine.

Then, feeling suddenly queasy, she shook him off. I'm just going to the loo.

She turned at the doorway and caught his eye, watching his face struggle to form an expression of concern.

The toilets were full of sweaty, swooning girls, limp as week-old lilies with the heat and drugs. Even the mirrors were sweating.

A large Nigerian woman was fanning herself with a battered copy of *OK!* magazine, dealing imperiously with the girls who came to scrutinise the table of treasures over which she presided: half-empty perfume bottles, lipsticks, brushes, lollipops – all laid out like artefacts from a dig. Genie dropped some coins in the dish and took a red lipstick misshapen by a hundred mouths, trying it on in front of the mirror. It drove like a wonky dodgem and veered across her face. She rubbed the mark away with a piece of tissue and inspected the damage. It looked as if she'd been slapped. Rubbing made it worse. She gave up, put the lipstick back and looked through the perfume. She picked a bottle at random and sprayed. The smell overwhelmed her and she ran to a sink and threw herself over it. The vomit came out in a satisfyingly clean motion, she thought, like film run backwards.

She rested her forehead against the mirror; it had the cold, invasive touch of a speculum. Her face was pale, but jammy around the mouth with lipstick. What a mess, she thought.

A girl filling a bottle with water at the sink beside her asked if she was alright. Genie explained that she had never taken one of these things before. The girl, who on closer inspection was actually a lot older than Genie first supposed, went soft-eyed.

Lucky you. Your first time. What did you take?

A pill.

I know that. I mean what kind?

A speckled one.

Never mind. Your first time, eh? Mine were doves.

Genie was pleased with the image: a speckled dove. The girl herself was soft and smoky-looking, plump-breasted like a wood pigeon.

Have you been sick, love? Do you feel OK now?

Genie nodded and closed her eyes tight as though inhaling deeply.

Ah, cooed the pigeon, that'll be the smack in it.

Genie thought in a detached way that the pill must have started to work: the idea that she had ingested smack was not as alarming as it should have been. And she was proved right when she finally left the toilets and a wave of clubbers broke around her and she was carried along the corridor and down the stairs, moving without resistance through the crowd, flowing down the stairs and to the basement dance floor, where she found Paul. He was dancing.

Genie tugged at his sleeve and he opened his eyes.

Genie! He grinned down at her, ruffling her hair.

Coming up is an elegant way to describe it, Genie thought, the nausea quite gone now and her blood turning to something like honey as she locked onto the bass line, tripping up on the sneaky breakbeats, feeling for the spaces in between. It's like skipping with two ropes, she thought, the way she used to do at school. She tugged at Paul's shirt, wanting to tell him she felt great, but the words burst like bubbles in her mouth and Paul had his eyes closed, lost in it.

After a while, almost telepathically, they both edged towards the side of the dance floor, to some sofas in the corner. Genie quite liked the idea of a cigarette. She asked Paul for one and he offered her his crushed packet.

It's your last one.

We can share it, he said.

He lit up and passed it to her. She took a drag, the ashiness in her mouth almost savoury. Once, when she'd been trying to give up, she had switched from Silk Cut to Marlboro Reds. Instead of being repulsed for life as planned, she had simply got used to the stronger taste. A residue of the repulsion factor remained and, if she thought about it, had probably become part of the pleasure of smoking for her now. But now the ashiness turned to cinders which left a burning in her throat. She passed Paul the remainder of the cigarette and swallowed some water from a small bottle in her bag.

Feeling better? he asked.

Yeah. I was sick. But I'm OK now. It wasn't really like being sick. It felt quite nice actually.

The word she thought of was 'rinse'. It had felt as fresh and cleansing as rinsing her hair. The word 'rinse' led Genie to register a vague thirstiness she realised had been building up in her before she'd even lit that cigarette. She downed the rest of the water.

Paul sighed contentedly and emitted a lazy smoke ring. He squeezed her arm; Paul, who had been so silent and moody lately. Now all that bad feeling had melted away. It felt right to talk to him.

You've seemed really distant lately –

But Paul was staring at something behind her.

Two ice sculptures sat on the bar, a male and female torso. The club was launching its own brand of water and the bar staff were pouring bottles of it into the apparently hollow sculptures as clubbers queued to drink through the genitals. He was watching a girl with long red hair going down on the ice cock, giving it plenty of tongue.

I thought that was Eloise.

He shook his head, as though trying to rid himself of the image.

Sort of thing she'd do.

They both laughed.

Just let me know if I'm cramping your style at any point, she said. You're a single man, remember.

What's the matter? Don't you like hanging out with your big brother?

It wasn't like Paul to be so sociable on pills. Not since the early days, anyway. She'd gone along with him to a couple of squat parties in recent years and after leaving him to go and dance would often return to find him sitting alone in the corner. He seemed to like the experience of overloading himself and just sitting on his own, breathing. Absorbing himself in the pleasure of breathing in and out. If you thought too hard about breathing you might forget how to do it at all, like saying a word over and over again until it lost its meaning. But this was like her fifteenth birthday all over again. How *he* had been that night. The warmth, the lightness. Taking this pill was like opening up a time capsule. *Swallowing* a time capsule. She'd taken it because she wanted to talk to Paul, to feel close to him, to have him open up to her. She remembered a film they had watched together once: about a man's search for his girlfriend who'd disappeared suddenly when they'd stopped at a garage for petrol. After years of searching, her abductor contacted him and agreed to meet up. On meeting, the abductor said, If you want to know what happened to your girlfriend, take this. He held out a pill, which the boyfriend took. When he came to, he found himself in a coffin.

Her thirst was more persistent than she'd supposed, Genie realised, feeling now as though she had a mouthful of sawdust. As if she were that character in the film and had maybe tried to chew her way out through the coffin. She reached for Paul's water bottle, and emptied it in three swallows. It had obviously been refilled several times, and was creased with tiny white scars where the plastic had been stressed. Handing it back to him, Genie realised that her hand was damp – that the bottle was starting to leak. Or had she broken out in a sweat without realising it? Her throat seemed drier than ever.

Genie?

She realised, as she caught him sneaking glances at her, that she probably looked uneasy. How long had she been drifting off like that? He was trying not to look concerned, she could see that, she could see he didn't want to trigger anxiety in her but he'd seen her looking upset. Walking past the school chapel at night with Eloise had been like that too, past the two candles lit in perpetual vigil by the chapel doors, their flames rocking in a draught that threatened to blow them out, heralding the presence of the devil, flames that threw huge shadows which licked the walls and followed them along the corridor, Genie and Eloise not daring to look one another in the eye because of the fear that would spark up between them.

Genie wanted to get away so that Paul wouldn't mirror and distort her mood into paranoia as he seemed to be doing now. Suddenly she felt sick again. She had drunk too much water too quickly. And yet her thirst, if anything, had intensified.

I'm just going to be sick now.

She said this in completely the wrong tone, it sounded to her – too bright or too casual, like *I'm just going to buy some more cigarettes*, but then she thought wildly, What would be the right way to say it? She couldn't remember how she would normally say it.

Shall I come with you?

Oh, no – no – I'll be fine.

I'll just see you back here, then.

She couldn't get away fast enough, pushing her way through the dancers, who didn't melt aside this time but stood solid as pillars, blocking her way as she stumbled past the ice torsos on the bar, the ice cock sucked to a stump, leaking sadly.

The pigeon girl was still there, standing sentry beside the sinks, a bottle held under the tap; she was reassuring a freaked-out teenager with eyes like glitterballs. Genie watched her jaws working mechanically like an insect's.

Don't worry, love, just stay with me, here have some of this water. This is your first one, isn't it, love? Don't worry, you just have some of this water. It's coming on strong now but when it calms down you'll have the time of your fucking life, love. Just go with it. Go with it...

She didn't seem to recognise Genie.

Genie ran to a sink and stuck her mouth to the tap, drinking in prolonged swallows. And now the nausea was quite violent, each gag washing her mouth full of thin, bitter bile that burnt her throat and dried it out. It was getting harder and harder to hold back.

In the cubicle, she sat on the floor, cradling the toilet bowl. She wished Paul were there to hold her hair back.

She didn't know how long afterwards it was that she left the toilets, but when she managed to find the place where she'd been with Paul, not daring to look into the faces of all these sweat-dripping freaks with eyes that wouldn't blink, staring at her as she pushed past, he had gone.

That was the last thing she remembered.

(xv) The Letter

It took Genie several minutes to realise where she was. The curtains were open, the bed made, the room iced over with moonlight. Paul's room. Dimly she became aware that she had been sleepwalking. She collapsed onto Paul's bed, pulled back the covers and crawled in. The sheets still smelt of him.

She awoke before Mam. In the kitchen, she made coffee and opened the dresser drawer where she found a packet of Paul's cigarettes and a lighter. Genie went onto the balcony. Out here all you saw was a grid of other balconies, each filled with their individual combinations of washing and plants, toys and junk. But if you looked up you saw a stretch of skyline that took in Canary Wharf, St Paul's Cathedral, the BT Tower and, if it was clear like today, the skeletal O of the London Eye. She took a cigarette from the packet and lit it. After a couple of puffs she stubbed it out in the dry earth of one of the potted geraniums Mam had put out there, hoping to create a Parisian-style balcony. But the plants were dusty and stunted: the place was permanently covered in a fine grey soot, a kind of light ash that might have been sucked up from some volcano on another island and scattered in the wind to fall here, in Hackney. Pigeons nibbled through the netting which Mam had hung up to keep them out and, finding nothing of interest to them, expressed disgust by shitting all over the place like vandals or occupying soldiers. Mam had given up on the balcony now and tried instead to cultivate plants indoors: fake-looking things with waxy leaves; their soil spiked with plastic care-instructions like medical charts at the end of a hospital bed. *Water sparingly. Needs constant attention.*

Mam knocked on the balcony door. She was holding up a letter. It's just come, Mam said. Mauritius.

Genie thought back to the letter Paul had sent half a lifetime ago. The address on this envelope was also handwritten, but the handwriting was unfamiliar. Along with a short letter written on thin, lined paper was a page from a book. It was a plate from *Paul et Virginie*. Genie recognised the image. The letter, which gave an address in La Gaulette, was from Gaetan, a friend Paul had mentioned before.

Paul
　　I found this on the floor after you left. I do not know if you will come back to Mauritius, and, if you do, whether you will visit me again. So I am returning this to your address in London. It looks valuable. If you are reading this then I am happy, because you are safe at home, where you belong. I think it is a mistake to go to Rodrigues.
　　　　　　　　　　Gaetan

Virginie on the prow of a ship, her eyes looking to Heaven, her hands clasped in prayer, her long fair hair whipped around her by a violent wind. The ship caught on a reef; a tempest raging. Paul, on the shore – stripped to the waist, his face contorted in agony, unable to reach her, restrained by two men on either side of him, one old and white, one black and middle-aged, both struggling to hold him back from the waves.

Mam did not like the idea at first.

Why should you go maxing out your credit cards chasing him halfway around the world? He left you on your own that night, Genie.

Because he is my brother and I love him more than he loves himself.

Genie told Mam all that she had learnt about Paul those past three weeks. Mam went quiet. Then she agreed that it would not be impossible for Genie to find him. Rodrigues was tiny, after all. But after the cyclone it might well be chaos there. And it was not possible to go directly from London. You could only reach it via Mauritius. Genie would have to fly there first.

Come with me, Genie said. Time you went back. We could make it a bit of a holiday. We could go and visit Grandmère.

She doesn't even know who I am, said Mam.

No, but you know who she is.

I won't go. Someone once said that to love your country you must leave it, and I did. But I will hate it if I go back. In a strange way I can understand why Paul would want to. He seems to have some unfinished business there. But I don't know why he's gone running off to *Rodrigues*.

Troubled souls seek the wilderness, said Genie.

PAUL

(i) Mauritius

Ten days after Cyclone Kalunde had reached a peak over the Indian Ocean, Paul, in a plane to Mauritius, was retracing its path. Up here, with only an indifferent sea below him, Paul felt free of everything he had left behind in London. He wondered if it would be possible to live on a plane, forever in international airspace. He thought of Grandmère, cut loose from the present tense. 'International airspace' was a less painful way to think about dementia.

Paul was drunk. But it was a reserved, self-contained kind of drunkenness – the only kind you could smuggle past the cabin crew. Paul had got drunk because of his fear of flying. That, and shame at his fear of flying, which to him signified a failure of imagination. Not fear of flying, Paul corrected himself. Fear of *crashing*. Then he thought *'smuggle'* and bit his lip to stop himself from laughing, thinking of the pills in his suitcase. It was strange to think of them all the way down there in the hold, but still with a hold on him. He had meant to flush them before boarding but had been too paranoid. After Genie's collapse Paul had determined to hang onto them. While he still had the pills, they could not harm anyone else. So he'd not wanted to let them out of his sight, out of his control. And then, after a while, he had begun to feel as though *they* wouldn't let *him* go.

After Genie's collapse Paul had run home to Mam's. Then he had run around his room, yanking at drawers, grabbing armfuls of clothes, groping for the tub of pills he kept behind the wardrobe, stuffing everything blindly into the small suitcase he'd taken from Mam's room, Mam's suitcase, the small cardboard one she'd carried through Heathrow in 1981 when they first came to London, the one he'd used now and again these past thirteen years, shuttling from squat to squat. The broken suitcase he'd had to tie a belt around to stop everything from falling out.

Hotel Europe, he'd thought, running to the bus stop. He could hide there.

As kids he and Genie had walked past it every Sunday on their way to Grandmère's. He had wondered even then about the kind of tourists who found themselves there, in run-down Hackney, on a major road where lorries thundered past heading for the docks and warehouses of Essex. The guests at Hotel Europe were Bangladeshis and Somalis and pinch-faced white people. They always seemed bewildered. They had never looked much like tourists to him. Then, when Paul was older, he would catch his breath as he walked past the place, thinking of the blonde girls in suspenders who wandered the rooms inside: it was a whorehouse, he told himself. It was the gauzy curtains drawn across open windows; something teasing about the lazy way they stirred in the breeze, at once inviting and secretive.

For a cheap hotel it wasn't so cheap, Paul discovered, though he suspected there were special rates for long-term guests. He thought he could guess who these were – they seemed defeated, no longer surprised to find themselves there. Paul unlocked the door to his room and, trembling, got into bed. It was already dawn. He pulled the covers up to his chin and lay there waiting for sleep. He lay there for several hours. He needed dark – unplugged dark – for sleep. Even when night eventually fell, it was hard to drift off with the fizzy street-light spilling through the curtains, soaking into the carpet; car beams tracked like searchlights across the ceiling, narrowly missing him in their sweep. Paul tried hard to think about Genie, about what might have become of her after she'd been stretchered away – but his thoughts evaporated almost as soon as he'd struggled to formulate them. Like blowing soap bubbles. But the memories – these came without effort. Was this how Grandmère felt? Today was his birthday, he remembered. His birthday, and the anniversary of Jean-Marie's death.

As he got older, Paul thought, sipping at another whisky, he felt he was hauling himself up through life in much the same way as this plane was climbing through the clouds. He would reach successive peaks of self-awareness from which he would look back down on his recent past and think, I didn't have a fucking clue then. And every so often he'd look back on the last time he'd thought that and think, God, I didn't have a fucking clue then... And so on, each step in this process of realisation corresponding to the increase in altitude, in age, in distance between himself and London, as confirmed by the blip-blip-blipping of the image on the little screen in the back of the seat in front of him. Paul wondered where all this enlightenment would end: possibly with his death, at the point of which he'd think, Fuck, I never had a fucking clue... He would reach death and the scales would fall away from his eyes as he crouched (his arms across his face in surrender) cowering and naked in the hot white light of absolute truth. He would feel like a baby. That's what we all are, Paul thought, looking at the sleeping bodies curled up in rows around him like the occupants of a neonatal ward: old babies.

But two women sitting near Paul were still awake. He heard snatches of their conversation: two Mauritian matrons who did not know one another, trying to work out how they were – knowing that they would be – connected. Perhaps they were somehow connected to *him*. Paul had heard many similar conversations throughout the flight. Creole, he thought, a Masonic handshake. That bastard language, formed from the cacophony of a hundred enslaved languages to confuse the oppressors, to hide things from them. Ironic, Paul used to think whenever Mam shouted at him in it, that it was the language of *his* oppressor. And it was still a secret language when it was spoken in London where few people knew it, as well as being a language for taking the piss out of people in, for swearing in, for being mad in, for cutting someone down in, for joking in, for being affectionate and playful in, for expressing love in. For Paul it was the language of love. It hurt to admit as much, because he spoke it, as Mam said, *kom si to ena patat so dan labus* (as though he had hot potatoes in his mouth); it hurt because Paul knew he would never speak it fluently, although in his dreams Creole came to him as naturally as dream-flight did. And when he dreamt of the two of them, him and Genie, as he had done constantly since leaving her that night – that same dream, the sad dream on the rocks that looked like chewing gum (she said) – the dream that he could never quite remember on waking – oddly and naturally enough, in the dream, when they spoke to one another, it was in Creole.

It was hearing Creole from two strangers that had made Paul realise he should abandon London for Mauritius. In the three days that followed Genie's collapse and his escape to Hotel Europe, Paul had not left his room once. Three days had slid away like sweat off Paul's back, leaving nothing but a salt stain on his sheets: three days and three nights he had spent there, lying drenched in his bed, alone. The morning his fever broke, he had woken with the certainty that if he didn't get out of London he would die. This in between dreams of him and Genie, each one ending with him saying something terribly sad that was not *Sorry* but seemed somehow to mean it.

During his fever, Paul had barely eaten. He still felt no urge to eat but he spent a long time looking at vegetables. Looking at vegetables made him calm. The vegetables outside the Turkish shop: onions, nestling in their grubby cardboard box; the ripe tomatoes hung tightly together, still clinging to their vines. If you touched the vines then held your fingers to your nose you went dizzy with the smell. What was it? Earth?

He pinched off a bunch and took them into the shop. Two dark-skinned middle-aged men – not quite Indian, not quite black – stood by the counter, chatting in another language, which Paul, registering the mild shock he always felt in these situations, recognised as Creole. Then, having run out of conversation, the two men stood nodding together. They both noticed Paul standing there with his tomatoes, staring at them. Paul knew what he must do. Where he must go.

Leaving the shop, he felt calmer. He looked wild, though, he realised, as his reflection swam up at him from the window of a parked car: his shirt hung off him and his eyes had hollowed out. He had not shaved in days. And he noticed the sky's dull glint, like the sheen on old meat: it was going to rain. London rain wasn't cleansing, it just shifted the dirt around. But Paul didn't move any faster as the first few drops started to fall – though everyone around him was rushing for cover: the dusty old black guys who sat outside the minicab offices, the hard white kids who pulled up hoods to hide skin like pitted cement. Paul didn't care about the rain. He didn't care if it turned him to mud. He didn't even care that, though it was still only March, there was already something warm and greasy, something second-hand about this rain which reminded him of the water that dripped out of air-conditioning vents onto the streets in summer – not water but the sweat of overheated office workers. Paul didn't care about anything except getting to Mauritius.

Which would mean seeing Eloise again.

(ii) March 2003

It wasn't the gunshot that woke him so much as the noises which followed: a car speeding away, a woman screaming, pausing for breath, then more screaming which seemed to segue into the astonished yelps of police sirens. He slept badly after that, his head full of terrible dreams about Genie. The next morning, looking out of his window, Paul saw ribbons of blue and white police tape stretched across sections of the road. Squad cars with flashing lights stood patient as horses while policemen nearby squinted into the middle distance, muttering self-consciously into their walkie-talkies. Bystanders watched and waited while kids ran around randomly like looters, working off their excitement. It felt as if a royal visit were expected.

Eloise was coming to see him. Perhaps she would think all this fuss was for her.

Paul lay back on his bed. He and Eloise had never stayed in a hotel together. In fact, he had stayed in a hotel only once before. A girl at his school used to sleep with boys for money. She liked him. She would do it for free, she said, but she wanted to stay in a hotel. She had picked one all the way across town, in Kensington. He'd had to hock his bike to pay for it. He'd ended up in Knightsbridge by mistake. Wandering around that area, trying to find the hotel, he'd felt as though he were in a foreign country. If you wanted to feel like a stranger in your own city, you just had to get lost in a part you'd never been to before, where you didn't belong. That was how he'd felt, looking for that hotel. He remembered the flashy car dealerships, the displays of oriental carpets for rich people to wipe their mud on. The Arab men in their shades and flowing robes, the Arab women in their shades and flowing robes, the liveried men loitering at the doors of hotels, all as transitory and featureless as the whorls of dust which blew disconsolately down the long blank streets. All the boutique windows slippery with a numb blank richness that looked right through you, and him, gawping, poor as a cockroach.

He had remembered that girl and the hotel again years later, the first time he'd gone to Eloise's house: her mother lived in that same part of town. He had gone there to rescue a drunken Genie. He had not let Genie down that time, at least.

He'd found the hotel in the end. He remembered the room as dim, the walls a dull shade of red, the colour of dried blood. The air was thick with stale cigarette smoke and dust. This and the slow pounding in his chest had made it hard to breathe. He had lain on the bed and waited for the girl. A few hours later he was still lying there alone, smoking the packet of cigarettes he had bought her for afterwards, watching MTV. He hadn't even felt like wanking.

And now he was back in that same hotel room, the red one, the air again heavy, and again he was alone. But this time, instead of lying on the bed and waiting for the girl to show up, he pushed aside one of the thick velvet curtains at the window and stepped behind it. He could see, in the large mirror opposite, just above the bed, that he was completely hidden in its folds. Again, he waited for the girl. But when the door opened it was Eloise who came in, followed by Sol, both of them panting as though they'd been chased there, the door slamming shut as Sol pushed El up against it. Then everything slowed down as Sol leaned in to kiss her. Paul realised then that he'd known all along they would appear there together. And, as he watched, Paul felt so jealous and so turned on that he had to bite his lip hard to stop himself from pushing back the curtain and joining them where they now lay on the bed, El on her back, long hair fanned out behind her as though floating in water. Floating in water: yes, he thought dreamily, sex in dreams was always slow, like floating, and as he thought this he realised that he was dreaming and, realising this, realised he was not fully asleep after all and that the thwump thwump thwump of them on the bed together was coming in fact from outside the room, someone was banging on the door of his room, the other hotel room outside his dream where he now lay, alone, awake and with a hard-on. Securing it with the waistband of his shorts, he slipped on his jeans and opened the door.

He didn't recognise her immediately. It was the hair. It was no longer the shade of dyed red that had made her skin look creamier than French butter. She'd gone natural, an indeterminate brown colour with an almost greenish sheen – the colour of sticks that crack underfoot in an English wood, he thought. It was bobbed, accentuating the little pointed chin that used to dig into his shoulder so viciously when he held her, as he did now, before she pulled away smartly.

Have I seen you in a suit before? he asked.

Not unless you count school uniform.

She came into the room. Sat down on the edge of the bed. Can I smoke?

Paul shrugged.

Put some clothes on, she said, not looking at him as she took out a packet of cigarettes, the menthol kind that teenage girls favoured, a taste she had never outgrown. She offered Paul the packet. Smoking them had always reminded him of Eloise: the actual taste of them – fresh and cold and hot and stale all at the same time. She looked around her.

Nice room, she said.

105

It is by my standards. I've only stayed in a hotel once before.

I know. You've told me the story.

You remind me of her, you know. The girl who never came to meet me.

His immediate thought when he'd first met Eloise had been that she looked as though she should have a tail. She looked as though she licked herself clean.

She was kind of feral like you.

Eloise fished into her handbag and brought out a brown envelope. This is what you wanted, right? I don't want it back. And I don't want to see you again, Paul.

I'm not planning on coming back any time soon. Thank you for this.

I have to get back to work now.

Where's your work?

Canary Wharf.

Ah. Daddy.

His company, yes.

I've only been there once. To Canary Wharf, I mean.

What business would you have round there?

He raised an eyebrow. There's a lot of business round there. But Paul had been too intimidated by the place to return. Some of the buildings he'd seen there were of a cobalt-blue glass, like the kind you looked through to view an eclipse. Perhaps you needed to look through coloured glass – emerald glass, grey-green glass the colour of the river – to see this place, Paul had thought, craning his neck to take in the Olympian heights of the buildings around him as he waited for the dealer who was coming to buy drugs from him.

I work in one of the tallest buildings there, Eloise said. Every time I go into it I remember a story you told me. The one about an ancient Greek philosopher who committed suicide by jumping into a volcano and how this other philosopher a few centuries later, some French guy, admired the Greek for choosing Earth over Heaven: *What an affirmation of love for the Earth!* Then the French guy was diagnosed with a terminal illness and also killed himself – by jumping from a building.

I don't remember that story, said Paul. Look at you. Job in the city. All smart. New boyfriend too, hey?

She nodded.

Paul got a soapy corrosive feeling then, as though his skin were covered in battery acid: a mixture of jealousy, sadness, lust. He had not had sex in such a long while that the thought of it scared him. In between break-ups with Eloise he would have casual sex with people he met in bars. But increasingly he'd found that the experience diminished him somehow. The effort of having to make himself anew for each encounter, after each encounter, made him feel as though he were losing pliability, as though he were – he'd heard this somewhere, about something else altogether, but he'd forgotten what – losing a little of the gold leaf from his photograph.

Paul leaned over and kissed Eloise. Hot ashes and mint. She pulled away.

Come on, Paul, she said gently. You know it's not going to happen. She reached out a hand, but her touch was cautious, as though she were touching something which might be very hot.

You've changed, Eloise.

Good, she said. When I was with you, I felt as though I was on the edge of the world; I felt like I was outside looking in. You made me feel like that. I loved that about you, I sought it out when I was young, but it scares me to be like that now. How can you live like you do? Why do you always want to make things difficult for yourself?

I just need to know that I'm alive.

Why do you have to be dead or alive? she said. Can't you find a happy medium like the rest of us? You wanting to run away from your mum and Genie, for example. What's that about?

Paul told her everything.

He told her about the night he'd broken his rule and given Genie a pill when she'd asked him to sort her out: how he'd refused and she'd pouted, said she'd take her business elsewhere, nodded at a bloke Paul didn't like the look of. How he'd said, Don't be stupid, he could give you anything; how Genie had smiled in a way that said, Exactly!

And so he'd slipped a pill from his cigarette packet and passed it to her. As she'd squeezed his hand in return he'd thought in a flash that it was all fucked up, him giving Genie this fruit of the Tree of Knowledge of Good and Evil when Genie – her smirk lit up by the strobe – was surely the snake here... Paul told Eloise about losing Genie, about finding girls in a back corridor, the girls with long lashes, high heels who looked like an avenue of spiky winter trees, leaning against the walls of the narrow corridor that led to the back room, at the back of which was a trestle table heaped high with coke. He told Eloise tales that made her nose water, of how he'd troughed at that trestle table, taking turns with the spiky girls, then jumped the queue until he'd felt sick with himself and everyone around him; how he'd left the place, left Genie there. It was while he was outside, striding up and down in the watery first light of morning, his body thrumming with power chords played on cathedral organs, that an ambulance had pulled up. He told Eloise that it was while he was wondering, Why not a back entrance for such eventualities, for the casualties, as they would for the VIPs? that he'd caught sight of the girl on the stretcher and seen, through the plastic mask clamped to her face, that it was Genie. And, before she could ask him, he told Eloise, Yes. I left her there.

(iii) Looking for Gaetan

The plane was about to land. The last time Paul had seen this view he'd been sixteen. He had taken the dark stains across the sea for forests of coral or seaweed fields. He knew now that they were in fact the shadows of clouds. Even something as insubstantial as a cloud cast a shadow. As the plane banked, Paul saw the sudden sweep of bay, that shy sort of turquoise, and felt hopeful for the first time in a long while. Paul was hoping that this feeling – this *London* feeling – would disappear when he arrived in Mauritius. He had lived with this feeling for a long time, he realised now, but it had become unbearable since the night of Genie's collapse.

But that feeling had not gone at all, he thought dully, as he stepped out of the plane and walked down the steps onto Mauritian soil, the heat giving him that welcoming hug, so tight it brought tears to his eyes. If anything, it got worse as he entered the terminal. It's jet-lag, he told himself. It's just a hangover. But it was neither of these which had shaken him up, he realised as he collected his suitcase – Mam's suitcase – from the carousel. It was guilt. Shame. Fear. It was the pills. Now, as he walked through Customs, slowing his pace to slow down his heart, a nasty dark mist of a hangover beginning to descend, he thought, If I'm to be punished for what I did to Genie, let someone stop me. Let someone pull me over. Look through my case. Open the tub of chewable Vitamin C tablets. Take one out and frown, call over a colleague.

But the Customs points were unmanned. He walked through unchallenged.

Paul had not been in touch with anyone but, even so, walking through Arrivals, he scanned the chaos of brown faces. He saw nobody he recognised, though in each of those faces he saw something half-familiar. That was how it felt to be in Mauritius again.

He could not recall ever having felt so oppressed by the island. The taxi drove along narrow roads shuttered by high-growing cane fields. Paul remembered the sugar cane, but it was the back of the driver's neck that brought Mauritius rushing home to him. That shade of brown. Almost reddish, like the earth barely glimpsed in the densely planted fields. And beyond the fields, eruptions of rock shaped like books flung aside, and dominating it all, even from a distance, Le Morne, like a petrified fortress.

The sky was full of clouds, the sun squinting through them, and the sea, as they turned onto the coastal road, was not at all the easy blue it had seemed from the plane. They passed shallow beaches where women stood in the water, hems of their skirts in one hand, sieves in the other, dipping them in the sea, sifting through what remained. Further on, by Pomponette, a group of schoolboys, skin blackened by the sun, were running into the sea in their underpants. Smaller somehow. Sadder.

The driver had given up on conversation back in Souillac, but as Le Morne pressed up against the windows he tried once more.

I don't need your ghost stories, Paul said. I know all about this place.

Neither of them spoke again until they reached La Gaulette, where Paul stopped the driver. He would walk to Gaetan's village from there.

On the road, he passed a stall where a woman stood hacking steaks from a big fish, weighing them on bloody scales. He nodded to her and she nodded back in the serious, almost formal way of country people here, who were wary of strangers.

Do you know Gaetan Pierre? Paul asked.

Oh, Gaetan. She shrugged disdainfully. You'll find him outside the shop.

Paul had not even considered that Gaetan might not be around. It had been fifteen years, but Gaetan would not have forgotten him. But Gaetan might well have believed that Paul had forgotten *him*. He felt a stinging shame then, remembering the letter he never answered.

It seemed even less of a village than he'd remembered. Just a cement-block shop and a row of *lacaz tol*, shacks of corrugated iron, some carefully painted and set in plots of well-tended land. Where the panels had been left unpainted you could see faded letters indicating former use – construction site fencing, mainly. A few men were squatting outside the shop, chatting and passing a bottle of beer between them. One of them, Paul realised with a shock, was Gaetan. They stared at one another for a few seconds. Then Gaetan, clearly drunk, ran over to him.

Caca Tibaba! He gave Paul the greeting he'd hoped for – the old nickname, the big hug, the slap on the back, taking Paul by the shoulders and examining him to see if he was still there, the Paul he knew, the little half-brother of his blood brother Jean-Marie, though Paul had been so young then. And perhaps this examination was a way to stop Paul from looking too closely at *him*.

Gaetan lived in the same *lacaz tol* set back from the road. But when he swung open the door – it was unlocked – Paul was shocked at the state of the place. The bed was unmade, the floor littered with copies of *Turf Magazine* and dirty plates, these last beaded with flies. Unwashed clothes hung limp from the back of the only chair. Some of the weave had come loose from its seat and stuck out untidily like stray hairs.

Gaetan waved an arm about. Nothing's changed. He smiled, slightly embarrassed.

Gaetan was well past forty now but looked older. His hair had mostly gone and what was left was grey and bristled. The whites of his eyes were flecked with blood and his face was bloated. His Manchester United shirt was streaked with something and he smelt of last night's drink.

Those horses you used to back – are they still running? Paul laughed, nudging with his foot a heap of betting slips on the floor. They rested on a pile of coins and crumpled tissues, the contents of a turned-out pocket. Paul put the bottle of Le Corsaire on the table, prompting Gaetan to disappear into the kitchen area.

There was a calendar on the wall above the bed, the kind that might come free with a Sunday supplement. The page was turned to January. January of the previous year, Paul noticed. It showed pictures of big grey Gothic buildings. The days of the week were in a language he did not recognise.

Where's this? he asked.

Helsinki.

Why have you got this up?

I don't know. Gaetan shrugged. He had returned with two glasses and a bowl of peanuts in their shells. It looks really foreign. Cold.

Paul knew then that he didn't need to ask if Gaetan had ever managed to leave the island.

A tourist gave it to me.

You're still playing the hotels, then? Paul asked.

Sort of.

Gaetan nodded towards the chair, which Paul took, while he himself settled down on the bed. He opened the rum and poured out two large measures of the dark, treacly-looking stuff. They clinked glasses and drank.

So, said Gaetan, wiping his mouth with the back of a hand and looking Paul full in the eyes, making it sound almost like an accusation, where have you been all this time? What are you doing back here?

It was a shock to hear a cockerel again. Paul woke up terrified when he heard it – that raw sound, its voice almost straining, breaking his sleep, a rude awakening, and then the dogs started, and sleep was over for the night. He had dreamt of Jean-Marie. The last thing he remembered them talking about, before passing out. Shortly after Jean-Marie died, Paul had spent a month here. But this time Gaetan had given up his bed and now he lay snoring on the floor, the smell of stale alcohol rolling off him in waves. Paul stepped over him, and went out into the back, to the kitchen area. His friend was a big drinker now, it seemed. They had worked their way through a whole bottle of rum, Gaetan tossing back most of it like lemonade.

Paul filled a pan with water and put it on the stove to boil. Walking out into the yard, he felt a freshness coming in from the sea. It was half-dark outside, the sky a faint lilac, still scattered with stars, and through the trees he imagined he could see the silhouettes of fishermen arranging their nets, dragging their *pirog* down to the water. He'd gone out there with Gaetan all those years ago and suddenly he remembered what a strangely beautiful and terrifying time it had been. But last night, when he'd asked about the *pirog*, Gaetan had just shrugged and said he'd lost the taste for being out at sea. Things were clearly not going so well for him: Paul had noticed a dead pot-plant in the corner where his guitar used to stand. But Gaetan seemed cheerful enough. He had even suggested a trip to Tamarin the next day.

Not tomorrow, Paul had said. There is someone I need to see.

Grandmère seemed to have brightened with age, Paul thought: her hair was a shinier blue-black and her blue-brown eyes gleamed in her brown skin. Or perhaps it was Mauritius that had brightened her. When they hugged, the flesh on her bare arms was like butter that had softened in the heat. There was something to be said for dementia, Paul thought: she carried herself with none of the shame he had noticed in some very old people, who seemed slightly embarrassed to still be alive. What age did Grandmère believe herself to be, anyway? He'd heard that in some cases the memories that came back to the afflicted were received as present-tense experiences; for some their memories stopped at a specific point in time. He'd heard of people who could not recognise themselves in photos beyond a certain age; people who could not recognise themselves in the mirror.

So! Grandmère said, patting the wicker sofa next to her. You are?

Paul, he said.

My grandson's name. She smiled, seeming to need no further explanation as to who this particular Paul was. She put her finger to her lips and nodded at the antique-looking TV. She was watching one of those corny old soaps he remembered from the last time he was in Mauritius: *Secrets de la famille*, made in Brazil and dubbed in France. He watched the last ten minutes with her, during which it was revealed that the master of the big house was the father of the young maid's illegitimate baby. When the credits rolled, Grandmère exhaled with satisfaction and indicated that he could switch the set off now. Then all he could hear was the heavy tick of a clock and suddenly he was back at her place in Hackney, on a Sunday afternoon after church.

114

Grandmère fanned herself, shaking her head. *Oh lo lo!* she chuckled. Always the same: two sides to every story and the white side is always the dark side. Just like my grandson's!

Paul, said Paul.

Yes, she said, beaming. Paul.

He looked around. This was not the kind of over-upholstered waiting room for death he associated with retirement homes in England. This seemed like a proper home. They were in the *salon*. The room was cool and dark. In the corner was a mahogany dresser, its marble top crowded with coloured glasses and *bonbonnières*; the parquet floors were highly polished and there were cotton lace curtains at the French windows, which opened onto a verandah overlooking a garden.

It's nice here, Paul said.

Yes, she said. But it's not Mauritius. I miss Mauritius.

Paul, looking out at the mango trees, marvelled at the power of a mind to deceive itself.

Perhaps you'll go back, one day.

Oh, no, she sighed, I'm going to die in London. You look a lot like my grandson, you know. What he'll look like when he's older.

How old is Paul?

Sixteen. Nearly seventeen.

What's he like?

Oh, difficult. She sighed again. His mother and sister are very upset with him.

Why?

He's run off to Mauritius. I lent him some money to do a computer course and instead he bought a plane ticket. Can you imagine! He lied to me.

Are you angry with him?

Not really, no. I can understand. London has never suited him. He came here when he was a boy. With his sister. His

115

little sister adores him. I must say, he is very sweet with her. My daughter brought them here from Mauritius six years ago when she left her husband.

Maybe Paul never wanted to leave the island.

You're probably right. If I think about how he was when he first came to London. Oh, it breaks my heart. One story –

Tell me, said Paul.

(iv) Grandmère's Story

The first time I ever met my grandson was at Heathrow Airport. He was ten years old. I had gone with my husband to meet them all, Paul, and my daughter and my little granddaughter Genie. And I can barely remember Paul there at the airport: while the rest of us were hugging and crying, Paul was standing on his own, hanging from the railings which separated the new arrivals from the waiting, swinging loosely to and fro, as though he didn't really care how he fitted into this new family, this new country. He was a very beautiful child. But this was of no comfort to him. He had left behind the only father he had ever known. But worse for him, I think, was losing his big brother. Jean-Marie was really Genie's brother but Paul missed him more. On that first walk home from the tube station, I watched how Paul looked around, registering just how different London was from Mauritius. That is how we learn to feel at home in a place: to notice what makes it different. Paul did not speak much at all, those first few days. We took him and Genie to the park, took them for walks in the neighbourhood. When we tried to draw him out, when we asked him what he thought of the place, he said, Where are the trees? Where are the dogs? In Mauritius there were many dogs. I remember them myself. They live in the streets and they all look bred from the same stock: skinny but jowly, dog-eared, slack-titted, piebald brown or black and white, or a dirty yellow colour. When Paul first came to London, he would obsessively draw pictures of these dogs. In Mauritius you see such dogs hanging around in the streets, taking themselves out for walks, snapping at one another in aggression or play. They have that sly, sideways skitter that street dogs develop, so that they never have their backs to danger. When Paul came to London that was what he noticed: there were no fruits hanging on the trees and no dogs wandering the streets. And then one day, some weeks after he and Genie arrived, the two of them were outside playing. When night fell they still had not come home and we began to get worried. When they finally came in, long after they were due home, their mother shouted at them. I asked them where they had been. Paul looked upset and would not speak. But Genie told us this story. They were out in the street when they saw a dog, a ginger dog. Paul said it was lost. Genie asked how Paul knew it was lost and Paul said, 'Cos it's alone: dogs on their own are always lost. But what about cats? Genie said. Cats are different, Paul said. She said, But why? and he said, Because. This dog belongs to someone, Paul said. The dog nosed around their legs and sniffed their feet. Genie thought they should keep it. I can just see her now, squatting down and throwing her arms around the dog's neck, kissing his flat, greasy head. Paul felt for a collar. He found a bronze disc on it that said 'Pieshop'. That's his name, Paul said. He lives in Camden. He must have been gone from home a while, he's lost weight: look how loose his collar is. Pieshop lifted his eyes from the pavement, his gaze shifting to and from Paul's. From some angles, Paul told me later, his brown eyes had an orange glow. Like Genie's. Then Pieshop dipped his head and licked the pavement. Do you think he's hungry? Genie asked. Yeah, probably, Paul said, but we don't have any money. We should just get him back to his home and then he can eat. Paul said he would take the dog back home and Genie said she would go with him. Paul refused, but some way along Brecknock Road when she was still trailing him he had to stop and let her catch up as he didn't want her to get lost. OK, he said, come, but you're not sharing my reward. I don't want any reward, she said. Will there be a reward? The address was one of those tatty terraced houses with basement flats on the main road where people walking past will throw down their burger boxes and crisp packets. They walked up to the front door and knocked. It was opened by an old man. Pieshop! He called out to the dog but Pieshop only cowered, so the old man climbed down the steps and grabbed him by the collar. Bastard dog's always running away. As he was closing the door, Genie asked if Paul could have his reward; that Paul had told her Pieshop's owner would give him a reward for returning the dog. So the old man disappeared into the house and came back with two oranges. There you go, he said, closing the door. What kind of a reward is that? Paul said, looking at his orange in disgust. It was the kind with thin skin that hurt your thumbs to peel. As they were standing there, they heard the man shouting, then heard Pieshop emit a yelp. Oh, cried Genie, that was Pieshop! Genie started to sob and asked Paul to do something. Paul shrugged. I can't, he said. He doesn't belong to us. Then Paul threw his orange as hard as he could and watched it burst and dribble down the old man's door. And then Genie threw her orange and it fell short and rolled away back down the steps towards them and they looked at each other and Paul grabbed Genie's hand and they ran.

After Genie told us this story, Paul broke down in sobs. The dog was trying to run away, he said. And I took him back. I remembered this story as soon as his mother told me that he had gone back to Mauritius.

(v) April 1988

It was Jean-Marie who died, but it was Paul who felt like the ghost. In the days following the funeral he wandered alone around the house, trying to walk through walls. Gaetan, who'd not heard from him in days, called round and was concerned at the state in which he found his friend. You're coming with me, he told Paul, and Paul, feeling no impulse to the contrary – no impulses whatsoever – did not object.

In the state that he was in – beyond desires – and with Gaetan's good grace, Paul might well have remained in La Gaulette indefinitely. But then, after a month or so, came a chance encounter on the beach. After this, Paul realised he should return to London.

At Gaetan's, Paul shifted from ghost to shadow. Lacking the ability to progress through the day unaided, he took to copying Gaetan's every move. And, since Gaetan rose every morning before the sun did, to walk to La Gaulette and drag his *pirog* down to the sea where under a pale violet sky he rowed out to the reef and cast his nets, so did Paul. And because Gaetan spent the afternoon squatting under a tamarind tree by the shop – the morning's fishing over, his catch sold – drinking until sundown, Paul did too. Paul followed Gaetan in tossing back rum in front of the television until sleep hit them; the day that followed played out in much the same way as the previous one had.

All this Paul did without thinking, or feeling, both intellect and sentiment overwhelmed by an almost hubristic and hysterical sense of physical self. He ached in a million places from his sleepless nights on Gaetan's floor. His head thrummed from the almost constant rain that battered the tin roof of Gaetan's shack – the wet season, drawing to an end, seemed all the wetter for it. He seemed to be permanently hungry, eating as though he were hollow and trying to fill the hole in himself. He could not pass a woman, pretty or otherwise, without the instant threat of an erection. At times Paul's senses were so overstimulated that they became wildly uncalibrated and he experienced a kind of transcendental synaesthesia, so that when he walked on the beach before dawn he would confuse for an exhilarating second the grit of wet sand grains that rubbed between his bare feet and flip-flops with the stars still pricking the sky.

Out at sea, Paul would fall into a trance. The sea, unsettled by recent storms, became more agitated by the day. The waves smashed against the reef and Gaetan's jaw would clench with fear. Gaetan took to bringing a rum bottle with him, on which he pulled more and more as the days passed, while Paul stared at rainbows in the spray, following without question Gaetan's instructions. They caught fewer and fewer fish.

The day before their last ever fishing trip together, Gaetan had taken less than half his usual catch. They were sitting under the tamarind tree drinking, barely stirring in the heat. The question of their diminishing catch arose in conversation. Then Gaetan, apparently changing the subject, asked Paul if he had heard about some islands of near mythical beauty close by, where no people lived and turtles made pilgrimages to lay their eggs.

No, said Paul.

There are no women allowed on those islands, Gaetan told him. But one day a fisherman broke this taboo and brought his fiancée – in disguise – on board ship, telling the rest of the crew she was his little brother. They reached the islands safely and found a lagoon where all was calm and you could find big turtles so gentle they let themselves be taken without trying to escape. Then all the men disembarked to spend the night on land. That was when the storm broke. It swept over the island. The men took refuge in the trees, praying to the Virgin and the saints as their boat was smashed to splinters by the maddened waves. Then a huge wave bigger than all the others rolled in towards land and tore up a rock where some of the men were sheltering, washing them all away. As suddenly as the storm had broken, the wind then dropped, the sea was stilled and the sun broke through the clouds. The men fell on their knees thanking God but they heard a mournful voice crying, *Aiyo, tifrere!* It was the young fisherman. His fiancée had been swept away. He had caused the storm by bringing his lover to the island. He dared not admit what he had done and could only cry out for his 'little brother'.

That's nice, Paul said. It reminds me of *Paul et Virginie*. You know, the boy losing his love to the sea.

All our stories remind you of *Paul et Virginie*.

And Gaetan sucked his teeth and finished the bottle of rum without speaking.

Paul thought of Genie, and how long it had been since he had in fact last thought about her. Then he wondered why Gaetan had told him this story.

The next day, they caught no fish. The waves were purple, the sky was swagged with clouds and the wind moaned over the heaving water. It's biblical out here, Gaetan muttered, casting his eyes aloft, Gaetan himself transformed for an instant into an Old Testament engraving as he was illuminated by a break in the clouds. Hauling in their nets, Paul caught Gaetan glancing at him in the same way he had at the heavens. Suddenly Paul felt bereft, as though with that

122

silent accusation Gaetan had severed the invisible thread which had fated Paul to follow, unthinking, his friend's every movement. This feeling persisted long after they'd landed, and that afternoon they drank their rum in silence.

The next morning, Paul woke to see Gaetan creep about in the shadows, before gently opening the door to leave.

Hey, said Paul. Wait.

You're awake.

He'd thought Gaetan had just been leaving him to sleep, until he heard the guilt in his voice.

I'm coming with you, aren't I?

Gaetan leant against the door and sighed.

No. It's better you stay here. You're like a zombie, man. I think you're scaring away the fish. And that heavy weather! It's like taking a woman to Saint Brandon. I don't want any more bad luck out there. Go out for a walk today.

Gaetan lived nowhere, really. That was, the place where he lived had no name. It was a group of shacks and a shack-like shop off the side of the road between La Gaulette and Le Morne, not far from the mangrove swamps. Setting out later that morning, the rain having stopped and the wet road steaming in the sun, Paul found himself taking the Black River Coast road, drawn south to Le Morne, to the huge mass of rock which reared up from the end of the island's southwestern peninsula.

Gaetan had been born in the shadow of this mountain. His family had lived in a village at its base, Trou Chenille. But the village was no longer there. It was a haunted mountain, Gaetan had told Paul. The mountain was riddled with caves and its rocky overhangs were not easily accessible, leading it to become a refuge for bands of runaway slaves, the *maron*. There were many myths about these fugitives – it was said they practised voodoo and killed any babies born among them to stop their cries attracting soldiers. This wild place was haunted with spirits and at night their voices could be heard on the wind. If you looked up at the mountain, said Gaetan, who never did when he was out on the *pirog*, you could almost feel yourself being watched by spirits hidden in all those dark crevices.

Following the road round to the north shore of the peninsula, remembering all these stories, Paul felt his chest constrict. His breathing became shallow, as though he were climbing at altitude. He felt a kind of oppressiveness in the air but no wonder, he thought: the sun was strong and the air was damp with drying rain. It was not the mountain, he told himself, walking parallel to its base along the beach, heading towards the end of the peninsula. It was *not*. He decided on a swim. Wading into the water, he launched himself onto his back, then lost himself in the unhurried blue of the sky. It was hazy out at sea: Paul felt as though he were looking at the world through plate glass, but so closely that his breath was misting up the glass and the world was disappearing. Then it started to rain and the colours of the sky and the sea were softened and blurred like a watercolour.

It was as he was floating that he noticed the rock a little further out. A cross was erected on it. The site of a shipwreck, perhaps. Maybe even the wreck of the *Saint-Géran*, Virginie's doomed ship. Had that sunk here? A gradual horror stole over Paul as he realised he might be swimming among the drowned, so he flipped over and front-crawled as fast as he could back to shore.

As he staggered out of the shallows, he saw that he was no longer alone on the beach. A man was approaching him. A *blan* with long, matted hair – dirty blond, the colour of damp sand. He was in his late forties, Paul guessed, as he came closer.

You're a tourist? the man asked him.

Sort of. Paul no longer wondered how people knew. But the man's own speech was hesitant, as though he himself were speaking in a language not his own.

See that? The man pointed out to the rock and the cross. Do you know why that's there?

Paul shook his head.

To mark where the slaves drowned. Some of them threw themselves off this mountain rather than be caught. He squinted up at it. People drown here all the time. Trou Chenille, he said. Caterpillar Hole. It's the name of the current.

How odd to map areas of sea, Paul thought. Like mapping the sky. Naming currents as you would constellations.

So no swimming here. The man smiled. You might drown. People come here to do that deliberately, you know. Is that why you're here?

When the man looked at him closely, Paul was suddenly gripped with the sensory meltdown that made him confuse sand with stars, and he wondered why the man's icy blue eyes weren't running down his face, melting like tears in the heat.

Then the man laughed. He asked if Paul smoked *ganja*.

Paul nodded.

Good, said the man, and took out a pouch. His hands were spangled with salt and sand.

Trou Chenille, Paul said. There used to be a village here.

Yes, said the man. My family destroyed it.

Tell me, said Paul.

The people of that village, the man said, were Creole. They claimed to be the descendants of the *maron*. Some people say the *maron* are a myth. To prove the existence of a disappeared people, you point to the things they left behind. We, the living, know the dead by the things they cannot take

125

with them. But cooking pots, utensils… weapons… nothing like that has ever been found here. And so some people declare the *maron* never existed. But they were fugitives! Their aim was to leave no trace or they would have been caught. Their very invisibility proves their existence. Those who deny this are people who would prefer not to preserve the memory of slavery. People like my family. Some *blan* claimed the land of Trou Chenille and kicked the residents out. My family bought some of that land. This all happened a few years before I was born. I did not become aware of it until I was a young man, and when I learnt the true cost of my privilege I rejected it. I live in a little shack now, in that woodland behind you. But I was born on a large and beautiful estate near the Black River Gorge. My father was born there before me, as were his father and *his* father and grandfather, our forefather having come to Mauritius from Brittany. Of course you know the story of *Paul et Virginie*. The man who wrote it was inspired to do so when he came here from France in the late eighteenth century. And my grandfather's great-great-great-grandfather travelled with the author, Saint-Pierre, on that very same ship from Lorient. It is odd when you read Saint-Pierre's journals. He found Mauritius inhospitably rugged and yearned for the pastoral beauty of France. And yet *Paul et Virginie* is his hymn to this island, which he presents as a paradise, while he savages his homeland. A man between two worlds, as I feel myself to be. Like many of his countrymen, my Breton ancestor had not intended to stay in the colonies for long, but his fortunes had been amassed at such a rate that he found it impossible to leave. Eventually, over successive generations the family shifted from being French colonials to French Mauritians. They began to feel at home on the island. Their fortunes flourished through the exploitation and oppression of the other islanders. We made ours peddling poison. Poison of the darkest kind, the whitest kind, which might as well be crystals of blood. Sugar! As a young man I left the island to study the chemical processing of sugar, which would enable my family to produce ever greater quantities of the stuff. But the place where I chose to study changed the course of my fate. I went to Brittany. As a child I had been told many stories about the place and I was fascinated by it. I was particularly obsessed with the story of the drowned island of Ker-Ys, fabled to be close to the Bay of Douarnenez, where my family had originated. Somewhere deep under the sea might lie an ancient island city! In 1965 I began my studies in Rennes and spent much of my free time travelling the region, surfing on the west coast, which I came to know intimately. It is a wild place and in many ways reminds me of Mauritius. Have you ever been to Souillac, down in the south of the island? Le Souffleur? No? It's a rock in the sea which got its name from the whistling sound the waves used to make when they rushed through it. But the forces which shaped the rock in that way have eroded it further so that it is silent now as all rocks are, and eventually the rock itself will disappear, as all rocks eventually do. The sea there is wild. When I am there, I think of Finistère in Brittany, and whenever I was in Finistère I thought of Souillac.

Paul was suddenly aware of the shushing of the waves as they crept up on him and retreated. The man continued with his story.

I fell in love with Brittany, and then, towards the end of my studies, I fell in love with a Breton girl. Annick. She was a student of political science and an active member of an anarchist Breton liberationist party. Through my passion for Annick, and for Brittany, I found myself drawn into politics. Annick helped me to realise the true human cost of my

127

privilege. And then came May 1968. Listening to the news of the Paris riots on the wireless, I thought instantly of the drowned island of Ker-Ys, my childhood obsession. There's a Breton legend that Paris was built in imitation of Ker-Ys (from *Par Ys*, 'Like unto Ys') and a proverb claims: *Pa vo beuzet Paris, ec'h adsavo Ker Is* ('When Paris is swept away, Ker-Ys will re-emerge'). Revolution and the resurrection of a mythical island were linked in my mind. Of course that was also the year that Mauritius gained her independence. I came to realise that my struggle was here. And so I left Annick, and Brittany, to return. There is not much else to tell. I got involved with a militant workers' movement here and fell foul of hardliners who were suspicious of me as a *blan* and a member of the ruling class. No matter that I had cut myself off from my family and their money! I was expelled from the party. Suddenly I was adrift. Afloat between two worlds. Once again sugar turned to poison in my life, but this time it was brown, and I found myself addicted. I broke free of that by coming here. I climbed up into one of those caves up there. I lay there sweating and hallucinating for seven days and seven nights. And, after that, I awoke. Free. But trapped. You remember those books from one's childhood whose young heroes pass freely between the worlds of reality and magic? They snap their fingers or climb into paintings and pass instantly into another realm. Then they reach adolescence and are trapped. Trapped in their own world. The realm of magic still exists, but they can no longer reach it. This is how I have felt all my adult life. I am stuck between two worlds. Or trapped in one and no longer able to access the one I long for. It is why I live here, on this haunted rock, not quite on land and not quite at sea.

After the man had left him, Paul walked to the end of the peninsula, to the hotel there. Approaching the concierge

behind the desk, he asked how he might go about making a
reverse-charge phone call to London.

My brother has died, he said.

(vi) A Box of Taps

They had spent every night so far drinking and talking, but neither of them had told the other much about his life. But Paul did tell Gaetan that he'd always planned to come back. Running back to London had been a mistake, he admitted, and he'd soon realised it. His sadness about Jean-Marie had been just as acute in London. Moreover, Paul had returned to a London which felt different. His own fault: things between him and Mam and Genie had changed because of his leaving them in the first place. Paul told Gaetan how, to fund his return to Mauritius, he'd registered to be a subject on a paid medical trial. That he'd been given a bed next to the man who would become his best friend. He did not tell Gaetan that the eleven-year friendship had been cemented by drugs the weekend after they'd left the clinic. Paul's first rave and his first Ecstasy.

To say goodbye before you leave for Mauritius, Sol had said.

But as 'You Got The Love' came on, the drug had kicked in and Paul had raised his eyes to the lights which pulsed like speeded up time-lapse footage of hot-house flowers opening and closing, and what he'd thought was, Hello. And a few days later, on a visit to Genie at her new school, he'd thought the same when she'd introduced him to Eloise. So Paul had lost the urge to leave London.

I'll get it out of you eventually. Gaetan smiled. They were drinking again, sitting in front of the television. Paul noticed

130

it was still covered in doilies. What was it with Mauritian guys and doilies?

I told you, said Paul. I'm here on holiday.

But why come back now? Yes, you tell me you have some money now. But forgive me, he said, looking Paul up and down, you don't look very well off to me. You've got holes in your jeans...

That's the fashion in London. Paul explained how, in London, the richer you were, the poorer you dressed.

That's crazy! exclaimed Gaetan. What's the point of having money and dressing like a bum? You must be rolling in it, in that case... but how did you make your money?

Paul was spared the awkwardness of replying: disturbing images filled the TV screen and both were momentarily distracted. It was footage from a local news report in India, being replayed on the Mauritian news. Some kind of python had swallowed a calf too large to digest and was now, to its apparent shock, slowly starting to regurgitate it, its jaws unhinged in a terrible grin; the calf, limp, a raw pink, slick with the snake's gastric juices which had dissolved its skin. Paul remarked, fascinated, that it looked as if the snake were giving birth to the calf.

This was interrupted by a newsflash: scenes of mass looting in Baghdad, and the storming of Saddam Hussein's palace. A man carrying a vase and fake flowers half the size of himself ran into shot, looking delirious.

Paul laughed. What's he going to do with those?

Then on the local news there was an update on the progress of a young Muslim girl who had taken poison, insect repellent, for some hazy romantic reason. She had burnt her insides with the stuff but was lingering on.

Sometimes, said Gaetan, we get news about London. Do you get news about Mauritius in London?

Sometimes, said Paul feeling guilty.

Gaetan mentioned the riots in Port Louis. You must have heard about *those*.

I think so. Remind me.

Four years previously, Gaetan told him, there had been a pro-*ganja* rally in the capital, calling for decriminalisation of the drug. Creoles who followed Rastafarianism were chief among those demonstrating, led by Kaya, the famous *seggae* star. He had been arrested for smoking *ganja*. Three days later, he had died in police custody. Head injuries. He'd fallen, apparently. Weeks of rioting followed. A state of emergency was called.

Did you get involved? asked Paul.

No. I wasn't around. I didn't even make it to the demonstration. Gaetan looked troubled by this. But the old gang – London, Chauffeur, Tilamain, everyone – they were all there. They even went looting. Tilamain grabbed this massive box. It was heavy and hard to carry, what with his hand, you know. There were some *gard* on his ass so he had to hide it in some bushes and go back for it the next day. He didn't even know what he'd nicked until he opened the box.

And what did he get?

A box of taps.

Paul laughed. Gaetan looked annoyed.

Taps cost money. He managed to sell the lot for two hundred rupees.

Gaetan shook his head and threw back his drink, and as he did so Paul could see his eyes flickering the way they did whenever he was rummaging through his memory for a story. But this time it was not a story. It was an accusation.

You think that's *funny*? A box of taps? What the fuck do you know? I wish I had been there. You know London got beaten up by the *gard*? I should have been there. But you want to know why I wasn't there?

Tell me, said Paul.

(vii) Gaetan's Story

I can see it on your face. Ever since you arrived, this question, stuck like a fishbone in your throat: *What happened to you?* Well, I'll tell you. It's not a happy story, brother. I had a pretty nice life when you knew me before. I had my boat, my friends. We'd surf, we'd smoke *ganja* on the beach, meet with girls. And I had my music, my *seggae*. Playing at the hotels. But over the years it all changed. And then I went to prison. Did you know that? No, you wouldn't. How would you? You never wrote to anyone. I sent you a letter once and you never wrote back. That London fog, fogging up your head. You forgot about us. Well, it all started to fall apart not long after you left here. In the end I lost my boat. Then came prison. After that I lost my job playing at the hotels. Oh, yes, I'm working at a hotel now, but I don't play music there. I once did a favour for one of the managers, so when I lost the gigs he said he could get me other work. But only behind the scenes. I had a reputation. I couldn't play for the guests any more. So now I clean their rooms. Sometimes, if people leave stuff behind, I keep it. Just stuff no one would ever notice. Yeah, like that calendar. I know it's out of date. How you're looking at me now, it's different from how you used to look at me. Back when you came here. You were, what, sixteen? When I was that age, younger even, I used to surf. Tamarin. That's where we were the first night we met, remember? Jacques who has the hostel there now – me and him and a bunch of friends, we used to surf that spot. Beautiful wave. A perfect curl. Seemed at the time that our wave would just

133

appear on demand. We'd grab our boards and paddle out. And it's the west coast, so evenings were the best. Riding that endless glassy left as the sun was setting. Man, it was good for the soul! That was back when there were no tourists. There weren't many of us. We had that wave to ourselves. Then one day a small group of foreigners appeared. American guys. They were surfers. They were making a film about surfing. A *blan* who'd gone back to France had written about Tamarin in some big American magazine so these guys had come to see it for themselves. We were suspicious at first. But we smoked *ganja* with them and they told us about the film. They wanted to show the spirit of surfing, how surfing was about being in tune with nature, and about the people you met on your search for waves. They'd travelled all over the world but had never found a wave like ours. They called our island *Santosha.* Peace. For them, Mauritius, our wave, was mythical. Mystical. *Santosha is not a place but a state of mind*, they said, and we agreed. You know Le Morne, how it gives off this dark feeling? Back then Tamarin gave us just as strong a feeling, but a good one. Yeah, *peace*. And these guys felt it. They were cool. Real surfers. So they hung out with us there for half a year and we shared our wave, our *ganja*, with them. Those were good times. And then the film came out. Gradually, more surfers came to see Tamarin for themselves. Australians, South Africans. A few Americans. Even then, it was still cool. They had that spirit. That surfer's spirit. We never had a problem with them. To come all the way out here, just to ride our wave – well, we were honoured. And they knew to share it, to show some respect. But something changed. We started getting more tourists to Mauritius. And some of them wanted to surf. They weren't the kind of surfer we'd known before. They turned up in all the latest gear – gear! There was never gear before! We just rode on boards we'd made ourselves. These arseholes dropped in on your wave; they didn't know how to behave. And then the *blan* moved in. The kind who'd never been interested in surfing before. But suddenly they started showing up on the beach, strutting about, pushing everyone around. Not so much us – the original crew – they would never have dared. Just all the tourists. We didn't like that. But over the years, the strangest thing. The wave changed. It stopped showing up as often. Changes in the weather, the form of the ocean floor, I don't know. The sands just shifted. Maybe the sea could sense all this bad feeling and was starting to retreat. Fewer waves. More surfers. Bad attitude. It started getting nasty. Do you remember that *blan* fuck you bought your weed off when we were in Tamarin the night we met? The rich boy? Well, his brother thought he was a big surfer. Those two had some nasty friends. These were the nastiest of the *blan* surfers down at Tamarin. They called themselves the White Shorts. They told everyone they owned the wave. How can you own a wave! They used to paddle out with knives taped to the undersides of their boards. Flash them in people's faces. Some of my boys had run-ins with them but not me. I'd stopped surfing that spot. Before this all happened I had only ever surfed Le Morne and One Eye a couple of times but after the scene turned bad at Tamarin I started going out there more often. I was never really comfortable on reef breaks – you've been out with me on my *pirog*, you've seen what a wave can be; you know about the sharks. But eventually I started surfing those spots because there was nowhere else to go. It wasn't the same. Then, after Jean-Marie died, something strange happened. I got the fear. I lost my nerve and got ground up on the reef a few times. I surfed less and less and eventually stopped altogether. I smoked more *ganja*. Started drinking. Over the years I got into the horses. Cards too. I lost the boat. And then one day something happened and I realised that this turf war over the Tamarin spot *was* my fight after all. Do you remember the anniversary of Jean-Marie's death? Do you mark it? Oh, of course you do – it's your birthday. Well, every year in the weeks leading up to your birthday I get especially drunk. The day of Kaya's pro-*ganja* rally, I had pretty much been drunk for three weeks straight. I told you I missed the rally – well, this is why. That morning, just before we were due to meet up with the others in Port Louis, I had gone up there with Tilamain. I was sitting in James Snack with him, eating *bulet*. The only thing to eat when you're hungover. In fact, I was still drunk. That's what my lawyer said in court, though how that was supposed to help me, I don't know. Tilamain was complaining about women troubles as usual, and as usual I was ignoring him. I was looking around the place when I saw someone I thought I recognised from somewhere. I realised then that I must know him: the man looked away too quickly. He'd recognised me, but did not want me to recognise him. I'll tell you who it was. Do you remember that time we were fishing on Grande Rivière and this new *gard* followed us down and gave us shit? He searched Jean-Marie then didn't have the balls to search the rest of us? Well, it was him, that *gard*. I was sure of it. I asked Tilamain. Yes, he said, it's him. Then he goes back to his boring story, can you believe it? I'm just wondering what I'm going to do about it, when someone comes in and joins this guy. You would not believe who it was. It was him. The fucking *blan*. The *marsan*. The wannabe White Short you bought your weed off. That did it. Hey, you, I say. Everyone looks up from their bowls, including the *gard* and his mate. Yeah, you. You're the *gard* that was hassling us that time at Pointe aux Sables, aren't you? And all of a sudden people stopped eating, their ears burning. Some of these guys were going to the rally themselves. That cunt wasn't even in uniform but now everything about him screamed *gard* – his neatly trimmed hair, his well-scrubbed face, his ironed polo shirt, the way he got up from his stool in such a panic he knocked it over as he ran out – followed by his mate the *marsan*. He might as well have thrown a match into a can of petrol. I ran out straight after them. I chased them both down the street but lost the *gard*. I caught up with the *blan*, though. I dragged him round the back of a garage. No one stopped me. What happened next – I don't know how it happened. I must have still been drunk. I gave that *blan* the kicking of his life. I had never attacked anyone before, not even Maja who'd been begging for a slap many times before he did what he did. But I sure laid into this fuck. I was dancing about on him like fucking Fred Astaire. I was almost thrown off balance with each kick, I put so much of my weight into it. He must have been screaming, making some kind of noise, but I heard nothing. When I had finished I was panting with exhaustion, covered in sweat, like after you've just had a woman. Like I had just come, rolled off him, and was about to fall asleep, I was that calm. It looked like all the life had been kicked out of this *blan* because I had put all of myself into the kicking of him. My trainers were smeared with blood. Then I felt my arms being grabbed. Two *gard*. And their weaselly little colleague from James Snack. I missed the rally and I missed the riots because I was in prison. Oh, the *blan* paid me back threefold for what I did to him. He had *gard* friends, remember. And do you know who his dad is? The name was spelt out for me when I got my going-over. Do you see that my face is not the shape it was? I don't recognise my own face in the mirror these days. I still don't know if it was the *gard* I really wanted to kick in. But I missed my chance to get him. For Jean-Marie. Those *blan* fuckers think it's their island. Whose sweat made their money? This island belongs to no one. And especially not to you. Everything went wrong when you came out here all those years ago, Paul. I don't know why you've come back. What is there here for you? I think you should go.

(viii) 9th March 1988

Jean-Marie and his gang knew that they were no longer so young. Already their nights were spent reminiscing about other legendary nights from years back. They liked to tell Paul these stories, but really they were talking to themselves, to their pasts. But then there were the nights when everything came together, and Paul knew these would be talked about in the same breath as all the other nights they'd told him about, the ones he'd not been around for.

Then came the night that ended them all.

It was Paul's seventeenth birthday. The plan was to go to Sainte Croix to pick up some *ganja* from a friend of Maja's. Paul and Jean-Marie were waiting for the others to pick them up. It was just around sunset. Pointe aux Sables being on the west coast meant they got the full force of it. If you sat on the veranda you couldn't see the sun setting, just the high garden wall and the trees and the sky above you, but that was what Paul liked: he liked the way the sky turned a funny colour, turned everything a funny colour, though you couldn't see the source of the light. The whole place was lit up in such a strange way, it felt as if something terrible was about to happen. But it never did: the day ended and night fell. That was all.

He and Jean-Marie had just finished work. It was too high up for mosquitoes so they could enjoy their beer in peace. In the distance they could hear the sound of the Hindu prayers and canticles being offered to bless the construction of a new temple, mixing with the sound of the *muezzin*, dog fights and dog song, and the frenetic beeping and squealing of mopeds as they zipped about through the narrow streets below. They watched the local dogs run up and down, cheering on their favourite as he thundered past: *seval lisien*, Jean-Marie called him: horse-dog. Another, Minette, looked like a doe, Paul thought. Because they were mongrels, they all reminded you vaguely of something else. Then Jean-Marie told Paul the story of his dog, Helena, a handsome Great Dane. Privately Paul thought that the breeds that were pointed out to him here as Alsatian or Labrador were not quite like the breeds of those same names in England. There was always some other breed, or a cross of them, lurking in the background. One day, Helena had been taken ill and Jean-Marie had borrowed a truck from work to take her to the vet. He had sat in the back with her, soothing her, while Maja drove. And then, he said, she took my hand in her mouth and bit ever so gently on it and looked up at me and I knew she was trying to tell me that she was going. And then, she died. Someone poisoned her, he said bitterly. There are some jealous people around.

Paul didn't quite understand why anyone would be jealous of a dog, or who would be so jealous that they would do such a thing. But then he thought, perhaps in the same way that English dog breeds were different from breeds of the same name in Mauritius, perhaps jealousy here was of a different species from the kind you encountered in England. Or perhaps it was not the dog they were jealous of. And then Paul thought, *Maja.* Maja was like these dogs you found in Pointe aux Sables, the ones that hung out on street corners with no fixed address, finding dinner and a corner for the night with one of the local families, who had so many dogs of their own they never noticed one more. Maja, an Ilois, had come over from Diego Garcia with his family as a kid (he'd once told Paul with some bitterness how the British Government – *your* government – had brushed them off their island like so many crumbs and tipped them into the rats' nest that was the shanty town of Cassis). The forced exile had broken up Maja's family and when, as a teenager, he'd hit a bad patch with his mother – his father long since dead – Jean-Marie, who knew him from hanging around the local garage, had invited him round for dinner. Maja had stayed for days.

Yes, jealous, Jean-Marie said. It's a sardine tin here. When you cram people in and they can't escape, they turn on one another. Do you know that *seggae*, 'Paradise on earth, but hell for us...'? Do you know why *ganja* is illegal here? No? Well, if I were a politician, the first thing I would do would be to ban something that makes people think about things, question them.

And then he told Paul about a recurring dream he had.

I'm running, and as I'm running I'm getting lighter and lighter and I don't want to look back.

Are you running away from something or to something?

I don't know. It's like when I'm driving. When I get to the edge of the island I just want to carry on driving.

On the way to Sainte Croix, to visit the *marsan* friend of Maja's, Jean-Marie asked Chauffeur to stop off at the shrine of Père Laval. They would be passing anyway, he said. The remains of Père Laval, a celebrated missionary, were supposedly buried underneath the plaster effigy of him which lay in state, seeming almost to float on a sea of candles in the dim little chapel.

Chauffeur whispered to Paul that if you touched him he would bring you luck or help cure sickness. No wonder Père

Laval was looking a little chipped. The paint was peeling off him. The way he'd been painted, he looked as though he were wearing make up, and as they left the shrine Paul sniggered and said this to Jean-Marie, who frowned. Paul could never understand this about Jean-Marie, how he could be so intelligent, so thoughtful, so damn cool, and yet have this respect for things, traditions, faith and so on – why didn't he question everything, or at least laugh at things, the way Paul did? There was an innocence about Jean-Marie, a kind of naiveté that made him no different from the others. It made Paul wary of him, made Paul look down on him at times, and left him a little sad, as though he and the person he liked best in the world would never quite get each other.

The area where Maja's *marsan* friend lived looked a lot poorer than Pointe aux Sables. It was full of zinc shacks but they looked different from the ones you saw out in the country; these were left unpainted and were not well-maintained. They did not stand in carefully tended gardens, but scrubby yards. Paul saw chickens pecking in one abandoned lot so full of rubbish it looked like a garden full of overgrown flowers. They stopped off at the shop to buy a bottle of whisky. A group of lads younger than Paul were sitting outside. They looked at Chauffeur's truck suspiciously as it pulled up. Their heads were all shaved in elaborate patterns that looked almost like barcodes to Paul. He wondered if the patterns meant anything.

By the time they got to the *marsan*'s place – another zinc shack and, like the others here, shabby and uncared for – it was raining hard. The yard had turned into pools of yellow mud. As they jumped out and raced to get inside, Paul saw that against the back fence was a stack of hutches full of rabbits. He doubted they were kept as pets. In London homeless people kept dogs for company, protection, a sense of dignity – you were not the lowest of the low as long as another life depended on you. He wondered if the rabbits in their hutches made these people feel better about the shacks they lived in.

They crowded in and cracked open the bottle of Long John whisky. It tasted of the barrel it had been stored in, and was so rough, Paul thought he felt splinters in his tongue. He did not feel comfortable in the presence of the *marsan*'s dog, Bad Boy, an ugly, muscular creature, nor of Calesh himself, who had the same stupid look about him and in his string vest was equally ugly and muscular. The conversation followed an almost formal, ritualistic pattern of compliments and enquiries. Paul's mind drifted off to the rhythm of the rain on the corrugated iron roof until Maja whispered in Paul's ear, Do you like her?

Who?

Maja nodded at a divan in the corner. Paul had barely registered the girl who lay curled up on it, watching television with the sound turned down. Maja had told them that Calesh's sister was a little simple.

He nudged Paul.

So you weren't staring at her?

No, Paul said, looking anxiously at Calesh, to see if he'd heard.

What, you don't like her? Maja whispered, with a sneer.

Paul tried to keep calm. In strip lighting, expressions were harder to read. The place looked alien. Calesh, like Bad Boy, was looking up now, having felt some tension in the air.

Well, of course she's pretty, but...

But what? You don't like girls?

Paul shook his head in exasperation, meaning, No, it was not like that at all.

No? He doesn't like girls! Maja announced to the room, with a laugh.

But I do. Paul said. But –

But what? And then Maja started to laugh.

The woman was about his mother's age. She had yellow-brown skin and a crooked smile. She patted Paul on the arse. The others stood outside hooting as she closed the door on them, saying, Wait your turn, I won't be long with this one.

It was another *lacaz tol*. The roof was leaking.

It's been like that since the cyclone, she shrugged. Come and sit down, she said, patting the bed. It was the only place to sit in the room. Apart from the bed there was a small table covered in faded formica with a pattern of roses, a wardrobe, the door of which was closed on a piece of striped garment, and a low shelf which seemed to serve the dual purpose of shrine to Our Lady and dressing table: it held a small statuette and some incense, and bottles of perfume, talc and make-up. When Paul sat down, he smelt damp on the sheets.

The woman took his face in her hands and kissed him deeply. It tingled: he guessed she had been eating chillies. It was a soft kiss. Everything about her was soft, Paul realised, as she took his hands and placed them on her hips. But not soft in a nice way.

She laid him down on the bed and peeled off his shorts. To his shame he had an erection, which she started to knead firmly. It felt good. She saw him squirm and said, Not yet.

She took a condom from beside the make-up on her shrine and slid it over his cock, and then, pulling up her dress over her head in one movement, manoeuvred herself onto him, rocking back and forth. He didn't want to touch her, but she took his hands and placed them on her breasts, which were large and slack. Her areolae were huge, dark. They frightened him. They looked like the fake eyes on butterfly wings, meant to warn off predators. And all the while she was grinding, gradually faster and faster, until Paul felt something tear inside of him and he came.

As she was getting dressed he lay there, dumb. He felt as though he wanted to cry, and he felt thirst and something like hunger all at the same time.

When he stumbled out, he turned to her and thanked her (she laughed), thinking, Why? Why thank her? as though she had done him a favour. Perhaps that was insulting, he thought: she had been paid, after all, the others having taken care of that. A birthday present, they'd said. But she had not been paid much. Paul thought of what little that money would buy in London and felt ashamed.

When he went out into the road, Maja was still sneering.

You were quick. She should have charged half-price.

Paul ran at him, windmilling his arms, and before anyone knew what had happened he had smashed Maja on the nose, Maja's hands flying to his face as though trying to catch all the drops of blood which now shook from him.

Then everyone began to shout at once: Maja, swearing at Paul, rushing for him, put his hand to the pocket of his jeans and in one motion dug out a flick knife and pulled it open. Some of the others were trying to drag him back, asking him what the fuck he was doing, trying to wrest the knife from him, and then Jean-Marie was leaning into him, saying, Cool it, Maja! Cool it!

By this time Paul had started to cry, and he was too angry to care, running at Maja, oblivious to the knife, screaming at him. Before he knew it, Jean-Marie had jumped between them, and for a second the three of them rocked back and forth, locked together in something like a hug, until Jean-Marie gave a cry and fell back onto Paul, a dark jet of blood forced from his neck. Tilamain tore off his T-shirt and tried to staunch the flow, but when Jean-Marie slumped back and gurgled, eyes wet and blinking slowly, unfocused, like a newborn taking his first look at the world, Tilamain shrank back, horrified. Paul, holding Jean-Marie, felt him drop, as though in a faint.

It was only then, absurdly, that Paul wondered what it was that Jean-Marie had asked of Père Laval.

(ix) *Articles de luxe*

On the bus from Gaetan's to Port Louis, Paul noticed the small roadside shrines. He thought, Who has died? They reminded him of the bunches of tired flowers you saw tied to lamp-posts on treacherous stretches of London road. But these shrines, he realised, were exactly that: little drive-by places of worship.

Mauritius was even smaller than it had appeared when he'd arrived more than a fortnight previously. Everywhere he looked, those same fields of cane, those same small cement-block houses, the pyramids of black rock cleared from the fields where the cane grew. The landscape seemed to be repeating itself. But Paul was leaving that night for an even smaller island: Rodrigues. Gaetan's words had shaken him. Paul had no wish to stay in Mauritius, but nor could he go back home. So he was moving on. The fact that Rodrigues still lay in ruins after the cyclone did not discourage him: he'd be left alone there. He could hide out among the broken trees and the people trying to rebuild their lives.

The previous evening, Paul had taken Gaetan out for a Chinese meal in Flic-en-Flac to say goodbye. Gaetan, still guilty from his outburst, tried at first to dissuade him. He sat twisting a napkin which bore stains that could no longer be washed out. But Paul had decided.

Those things you said. You were right. I should go. But before I leave, there is someone I want to see.

Before you go, said Gaetan, I want to know. Why did you come? What happened in London?

146

Paul had always thought of Gaetan as a simple man, and sometimes, even, a stupid one. Paul thought this because there were times when he said things that Gaetan appeared not to fully understand. Now Paul was at a loss to offer any kind of explanation, or, at least, one he thought Gaetan might understand. He realised that although he could be quick-witted in Creole, bantering and bartering in it, he lacked sufficient fluency for the language he needed now. Or perhaps it wasn't the language he was lacking. All he could think of was, *mo onte*, I'm ashamed.

And after he'd told Gaetan the full story, of how he had just run away and left Genie there, Paul had said to Gaetan, *Mo onte*. And Gaetan had said nothing, and couldn't even meet his eye. He understood shame, at least.

At first, the capital seemed not to have changed much. At the bus station, the buses looked as clapped-out, the terminus as pot-holed, the pavement as cracked as he remembered. Walking through the city's heat – more intense here than on the coast – Paul recognised the ornate dilapidation of old colonial buildings, and the shabby little old-fashioned shops with signs in faded, fancy-lettering advertising *articles de luxe*. Luxury items. In fact they sold exercise books, brooms, skipping ropes, buckets, washing lines, footballs, shoe polish, beauty creams, tinned cheese, hair dye.

The same produce was being sold in the bazaar with the same patter: the pyramids of chillis green as vipers, the milky blue glasses of *aluda*. But here in Port Louis, Paul noticed, people spoke French to you now. Creole had become the language of intimacy. It was offensive to speak it to someone you didn't know. And set back from the road, behind professional fencing, he noticed more new buildings in the commercial district, shiny plate-glass tower blocks with mirrored surfaces – almost as tall, but not quite, as the royal palms which lined the central avenue stretching down to the new waterfront development, Le Caudan.

Le Caudan was where he was going. There he passed through colonnades of shops that sold real *articles de luxe* – duty-free jewellery, exquisite pieces sculpted from local wood. It was odd to think of Maja here. But this was where he worked now. Gaetan had not understood Paul's need to see him. Paul did not understand it fully himself. Thinking about it now, he guessed he wanted to know if that night had changed Maja's life irrevocably – changed Maja – the way it had changed him. As for the others – Chauffeur, London, Tilamain – when he thought of them as they were when he'd known them, he could imagine them running riot in the air-conditioned corridors of this place, laughing at all the expensive tourist trinkets, eyeing up the designer watches and hi-tech gadgets with a kind of juicy, vital envy. But if he thought of them as they probably were now, he did not like to think of them here. They would look awkward, shabby, slightly apologetic. A bunch of guys in their late thirties, early forties, married probably, with their wives and their sweaty vests, their pirate DVDs of dubbed American action movies, their football pools, their fly-swats and their Saturday bets during the turf season. He was scared to see them. He was scared of their disappointment, their resentment: that someone with his opportunities should have squandered them so royally. And he was scared that they would be as fucked-up as he was. There were relatively few ways to get fucked-up in a country this small, but it was possible: he did not want to see if they had turned to drink or to horses, to drugs or to loan sharks; if their wives, their families had turned their backs on them. He did not want to know if they were unemployable now because the kinds of jobs that were plentiful these days were what they would have seen as women's work – jobs in hotels, in textiles. Or

148

work that was for skilled people. Educated people. How could he face them, with his privileged life, as they always saw it – with his chance to see the world, his freedom to love whomever he wanted to love?

Mauritius had corrupted him: he had come to this tiny island and he had felt like a giant, or a man at least, though he saw too clearly now that he had only been a boy. Paul had felt, when he left them, a sense of being old before his time. He'd believed when he'd gone to London that there he really could do anything, really could go anywhere. And in the face of all that opportunity, that *responsibility* – he'd been paralysed.

At Burger World, Paul joined the queue to be served. When the Chinese kid behind the counter asked what he wanted, he asked to see Maja. The kid called out to the kitchen. Maja – an older, slower, more dishevelled Maja in a Burger World baseball cap and apron – appeared in the doorway. Saw Paul. Almost gasped.

I'm leaving for Rodrigues tonight, Paul said. I'm on my way to the port. But I wanted to see you.

Maja took off his apron, lifted the counter and came through. He led Paul to a free table which was shaped like a toadstool, the seats shaped liked smaller toadstools.

I often thought about writing to you, Maja said. To explain why things happened the way they did. Why I was the way I was. But now you are here, Maja said.

Tell me, said Paul.

149

(x) Maja's Story

I saw a film once. I forget the name. In it, a soldier, an American soldier, goes AWOL during the Second World War. He is hiding on an island in the South Pacific. On this island, children play freely. They swim and they fish and they laugh. The people are beautiful. Happy. Everyone has enough to eat. Everyone shares. They sing. It's the most beautiful singing. The soldier thinks he's found Paradise. That was what it was like on my island. That was the life I knew until I was six years old. I lived in a small cement house near the sea with my father, and mother and my twin sisters, Marie-Laure and Giselle. You didn't know I had sisters, did you? And my dog, Fusette. We called her Fusette because she was shaped like a little rocket. Me and Fusette went everywhere together. She used to swim in the sea and catch fish for me! You wouldn't believe what that dog could do. Then one day, when I was six, everything changed. One of the twins, Marie-Laure, got sick. My father took her to Mauritius to get her seen by the doctors there. But, like everyone who had travelled over on that ship, they never came home. Once they arrived in Mauritius, they were told they no longer had the right to return to the island. To live on it. None of us did. It was a time of great anxiety and confusion. We were all told that we would have to leave. No one wanted to go. But then the ship that used to bring our supplies – all the things we couldn't make or grow for ourselves on the island – stopped coming. It was as though the outside world had forgotten about us. People started arguing over things they would not have argued about before. There was a breadfruit tree in our neighbour's garden. We used to help ourselves to the fruit which grew on the branches overhanging our garden. But now the neighbour started complaining about this. She was an old woman who lived alone. We often helped her out with things. Fetching wood, sharing our catch, and so on. She said the tree belonged to her and we weren't to eat the fruit on it. But she could not have eaten all that fruit herself, never mind collected it! My mother got angry and said if that was how she was going to be then we would not want her fruit, which would taste bitter to her anyhow. So we were forbidden to touch the fruit, which went ungathered and fell off the tree and rotted into the ground. And all this time my father and Marie-Laure were still in Mauritius. We had no news of them. We were worried for Marie-Laure's health, besides. It was around this time that we started seeing strangers on the island. White men in uniforms, with charts and instruments. They would smile at us kids but we were afraid of them. And shortly after the men arrived, the dogs began to disappear. One day, I was out on the beach with Giselle and Fusette. Fusette just darted up the shore to something which looked like a washed-up log. She started circling this log, crouching low and howling. We ran to look. It was Hector, a neighbour's dog, a very handsome Alsatian. When I tried to take Fusette away from this awful scene she bit me. She had never bitten me before. After that, the bodies of more and more dogs began to turn up, bloated and fly-blown. They had been poisoned. We were told by these officials – the white men in uniform – that arrangements were being made for us to leave the island. We were angry about this. But then came one terrible night. I will never forget it. My mother had refused to let me play out that day. I snuck out into the yard anyway to take Fusette her rice – our dogs ate what we ate – but she was not there. Before all this, we had let her run free, like all the other dogs of the island. But during this time we had kept her tied up in the yard so that she would not disappear like the others. But now she was gone. I wanted to go looking for her but my mother would not let me. I cried and screamed. My mother slapped me. She had never hit me before. She said it was not like how it was before. Things were changing. It was too dangerous for me to be out on my own. Strange things were happening. I was sent to my bed where I just cried and cried, imagining what might have happened to Fusette. I must have sobbed myself to sleep because I woke in the middle of the night. I had had a nightmare. And as I gradually became more awake I realised with a growing horror that the terrible sounds I had heard in my sleep were coming from outside, from reality, and not from my bad dream. It was a howling, a terrible howling, of many, many dogs. And one of them, I know now, would have been Fusette. It was the British Government who ordered the rounding-up and the gassing of our dogs. It was the US Navy who did it. No, not the Navy. Members of the Navy. Young men, younger than we are today. Men like the soldier in that film. Men who probably liked dogs themselves. Who might even have grown up with dogs, or had them back home. It was these men who slaughtered our dogs, and how they could do it I do not know. After that, no one resisted the orders to leave. We were allowed one suitcase per family. We didn't have much but most of us had more than could fit in a suitcase. My father had made me a kite. Such a pretty thing. I had to leave it behind. He will make you another one, my mother promised. A better one. If there was one consolation in all this, it was that we would be reunited with Papa and Marie-Laure after almost a year apart. I don't know if I can impress upon you – I certainly couldn't fully conceive it at my young age – the enormous pain of standing on the deck of a ship, watching your island recede from view, not knowing when you will see it again. Of course, never, for some who died shortly after we got to Mauritius. And never, we were told by the British Government. But we could not think 'never' as we watched it disappear from view until all we could see around us was the sea, which is like saying the middle of nowhere. It was a horrible journey. We slept on bags of birdshit in the hold, listening to the horses on deck. They sounded terrified. They made a terrible sound. But we were strangely silent. In shock, I think. We were offloaded in Mauritius, and taken to our new home. I almost laugh to think about it now, but if I could imagine a place that was the exact opposite of our island, it was the place they took us to. An abandoned estate. More like a barracks. No glass in the windows, no water. Filth in all the rooms. Rats, cockroaches. A prison. As if we were being punished for something. And the man who came to meet us there, my father, was no longer my father. Not the man I recognised. He had grown thin. He was so painfully thin that it seemed to me as he walked towards us that he was in pain, as though his bones which stuck out of him like knife blades cut him up as he walked. He smelt strange to me. Marie-Laure was dead. She had been very sick. They had given her medicine for the pain and after she had died my father had taken what was left of it for *his* pain. And this thing which was all he was living for now was killing him. Giselle died soon after we arrived. She had what we came to call *sagren*. It's a word that means sadness, regret. It eats you up inside. It turns you into a shadow. We never saw my father much, after that. Me and Mam moved from the prison to a place in Port Louis. The night Jean-Marie died, when we went to visit the *marsan*, do you remember? Do you remember the miserable state of his place? We lived in a place worse than that. But my mother didn't seem to care. She didn't seem to care about anything by then, not even me. Do you remember the woman from that night? The whore we paid to have sex with you? That is what my mother did. What she became. A shadow, I tell you. I am one of the lucky ones. In prison, I found Allah. Or he found me. And now I know a kind of peace. I do not touch alcohol, I do not touch cigarettes, I do not touch *ganja*, I do not touch women. But you, I can see *sagren* in you. You are not the boy you were. I know why you've come looking for me, after all that happened. After what I did to you. I took your brother. Allah has sent you to me. So I can look you in the eye and ask your forgiveness, and tell you to open your heart to Allah, and become *my* brother. That is the only way I can make amends for what I did to you.

(xi) February 1988

The first time Paul met Gaetan was at Tamarin. Gaetan had never really been part of Jean-Marie's regular crew: he was a surfer and had his own friends. And he was a fisherman, a country boy, living south. But he was a cousin of one of the gang and Jean-Marie had always liked him. Gaetan rarely came up to Port Louis, but every now and then they'd all head down to La Gaulette to meet up with him, to swap beer and *ganja* for some of his catch, which they'd cook up on the beach. Paul met him the day Chauffeur got his truck and drove them all down to the beach.

It was a Saturday. Paul and Jean-Marie and some of the others were helping a neighbour build a terrace on his roof. Most of the roofs in Pointe aux Sables were flat and looked unfinished, with rods poking up out of the cement, left like that to give their owners the option of extending upwards when the money was available. But then there were newer houses, built with pointed roofs in the Western style.

What a statement to make to the world, Jean-Marie had said to Paul, pointing these out. That you have reached your potential for growth.

Work was finished for the day and they sat around sharing a bottle of beer. Maja took a swig, then spat it out.

If I'd wanted a hot drink I would've had tea.

Jean-Marie laughed and took the bottle from him.

If we'd done things my way, he said, we would have finished quicker and this wouldn't have had time to sit around sunbathing...

Maja took a spent match from the floor and started to prod at a millipede crawling by his flip-flop. It avoided his attentions, executed an elegant feint and rippled away. He flicked the match at it. Paul was still looking at the millipede – impressed by its economy of movement – when he heard a truck pull up outside the house. An unfamiliar horn sounded. Maja looked down.

Well, fuck me! Chauffeur's got his *transporte*!

Most of Jean-Marie's gang, his friends and cousins, had two names: their birth name and another acquired once people had worked out who or what they were:

– Chauffeur was *Chauffeur* because he was a bus driver.

– London was *London* because he had been there once and talked of it often (Where did you stay? Paul had asked, and London, raising bulging eyes to the sky, had said dreamily, Croydon...).

– *Tilamain* was born with an unformed hand.

– *Maja* meant 'crazy fun'. Paul never did find out what his real name was.

– And Jean-Marie was sometimes known as *Zanblon* because he was as purple-dark and neatly made as the fruit itself, and Paul secretly thought that his personality had a sharp, complicated flavour too. They liked to complicate the flavours of their fruit, these Mauritians: if you stopped on the street at a bike-kiosk – a glass case attached to the back of a moped, the case stuffed with *zanblon*, *goyav desin*, slices of small Victoria pineapple – you were offered with your fruit a twist of paper filled with pinkish powder, like sherbet, to dip it into. It wasn't sherbet though but *disel piman* – a mix of chilli powder and salt. The colour of the earth in the cane fields.

Until that Saturday, it had felt to Paul as though he and the gang were always running around looking for something – *ganja* or transport or beers or money or girls or a radio station playing good *seggae* or sometimes just one of the others. So when Chaufffeur got his truck everything changed: one less thing to look for, and something to help them go looking for everything else they needed. It was a sweet little Toyota flat-bed in good nick – only two years old, with 60,000km on the clock and a decent stereo. It was smart, too: glossy black paintwork and an aquamarine trim. They circled it, squatting down to examine the tyres, rapping a couple of times on the body to check out how it sounded. They smiled at each other in approval, though only Jean-Marie was a mechanic. Then they unhooked the tail of the truck and sat on it. They peered through the open window into the driver's cabin and turned up the volume on the stereo.

Jean-Marie said, So where are we going?

Tamarin, said Maja. Let's go find some *ganja*.

Yes, said Jean-Marie. Gaetan will be there.

They all piled in and Chauffeur floored the accelerator. He slammed the horn whenever they passed a group of girls. They barely glimpsed faces, he drove that fast. Paul was glad to be sitting by the window, so he could lose himself in the view.

Paul had been out there almost four months already, but still he took delight in all the snack shacks, the lovingly hand-painted signs, the bushes of bougainvillaea like squashed-up boxy Chinese lanterns, the mixed look of the people, the mixture of races, which was so new, so fresh still, that you could if you wished disentangle them – the Creole from the Chinese, the European from the Indian. But sometimes you could stare for a long time without really being able to tell until the last minute, until a face turned, an expression formed, and from the corner of your eye some Indian or African or Portuguese or French or Dutch turned and

157

slithered away as suddenly as it had been glimpsed. The way *all* of it was a mixture of half-familiar from childhood, and foreign after London.

Paul felt as though what rolled past his window were a film, with the car stereo as a soundtrack. They were listening to The Clash and the music seemed just right to Paul: nostalgic music for the others, who were reminded of a time when they had been as young as Paul was now, ten days shy of his seventeenth birthday. It was so English, that sound, so *London*, pulling him in another direction, which was the way Paul thought he liked things best then, being slightly between two worlds. But every now and again his eyes would go unfocused and he would not see Mauritius: these were the times when he was thinking of Genie, and of how much he wanted her to be here with him. It was as though he could not hold them both – Genie and Mauritius – in his mind at the same time.

The *marsan* was a rich *blan*, his father a lawyer for one of the big sugar companies. He looked up at them and nodded as Paul and Jean-Marie walked into the bar. Paul saw him draw back a little, saw him notice that Paul wasn't Mauritian, the way everyone seemed to know, though how, Paul couldn't tell. And perhaps that was the position of the foreigner, Paul thought: never quite understanding what it was about him that marked him out as foreign.

Jean-Marie greeted him and introduced Paul.

You French? the *marsan* asked him, in French.

I'm English, Paul replied, in Creole.

And so they chatted in Creole for a bit about England, its football teams, its weather. Marcel – that was his name – asked if Paul was a student. Paul replied that he was not. He'd left school, he said, and now wanted to make a life for himself here.

And you? Paul asked.

I'm a fisherman.

Paul must have given him a funny look – Marcel must have seen him take in the white-gold skin, the designer surf T-shirt and slack unmuscled arms – because he added, A planter too. Also, I make things out of shells.

Nice life, Paul said.

Yeah, Marcel said. It would kill him to work in an office. Wearing a suit and tie and all that. Every time he put on a tie – for weddings or funerals or whatever – he thought he was going to choke.

On their way back to the beach to hook up with the others, Paul said, That bloke. He didn't seem like a fisherman to me.

Fisherman? said Jean-Marie. All that guy fishes for is money from his mother's handbag. He's not doing anything with his life except waiting for his parents to die. You'll meet Gaetan. He's the real deal.

It's still odd to me, Paul said, hearing a white guy speak Creole.

Well, he's Mauritian. But his first language would be French. That's what he'd speak at home. Guys like that, they're the first to pick up all the new slang in Creole. Guys like that say *mari* and *bugla* a lot. He's a cunt. Him and his brother. They're always having run-ins with Gaetan's lot. Surf business – don't ask me. Turf wars over this place. His *ganja* is good, though.

And sure enough Gaetan was there that night at Tamarin, with his surfer friends. He had built up a fire and sat tending it, sitting apart from the rest of them, smiling shyly at Paul now and then.

You see how different these country people are from you and me? Maja whispered. Even then Paul had felt uncomfortable with the conspiratorial way in which he spoke. He did not like Maja implying that he and Paul thought the same way. After Jean-Marie's death, Paul would come to learn that Gaetan's silence and distant smile were typical of the fishermen here – as though they spent too long staring out to sea.

Gaetan picked up his guitar and started to play, his friend accompanying him on a jerry can filled with sand. They sang a *sega*, 'Roseda', Maja explaining the lyrics to Paul. A man imploring his beautiful young wife to stop the drinking that was destroying her. Maja, so fond of sneering, seemed to be genuinely moved.

And there, on the beach, through a rain so fine it looked like smoke, the moonlight was almost blue. You saw the sea stretch out to the west but then – how could Paul explain this? – it just stopped. There must have been a mist down but you couldn't tell, you couldn't see anything. It looked like the end of the world, Paul said.

Like an apocalypse? Jean-Marie asked, passing him the coconut bong.

Paul took another warm, fragrant lungful.

No, he said, almost sighing as he exhaled. Like the world ends here.

(xii) Rodrigues

It took a day and a night for Paul to reach Rodrigues. He took a seat on deck near two men – a heavily freckled Chinese man and his gaunt Creole friend – who were passing a bottle of rum between them. He heard them talking about the Muslim girl who had poisoned herself, the one who'd been mentioned on the news at Gaetan's. Paul learnt that she had died after a long and painful struggle. Noticing that he was listening, the men passed the bottle to Paul. There were a lot of suicides in Mauritius, they said. Nearly every week there was a story of a poisoning, a hanging, a leap into the void or sometimes a drowning, possibly not accidental. The reasons given never seemed reason enough, they said: debt, divorce, unemployment, bereavement. What reason do you need? Paul asked. In order to consider taking that step it was enough just to be ambivalent about life. The Creole man told him with no bitterness that without money, without education, without talent, without somehow managing to stow away – on someone else's passport, say – if you were poor and likely to stay that way, suicide really was the only way of getting off this island, if you weren't prepared to wait around for death.

The two men were Mauritians. At first they described themselves as businessmen. They had been detained in Mauritius because of the cyclone, they said, but were now happy to be able to return to their business in Rodrigues. Paul thought better of asking for further details. But once they were drunk they confided in him the nature of their

161

enterprise. Prospecting, they said. There was treasure on that island. Pirate treasure. It had never been found. It was the cyclone that had drawn them. The devastation wreaked might well have unearthed what had lain buried. They were like those people who combed the rocks after shipwrecks, Paul thought.

They brought out a pack of cards and invited him to play. He shared the rest of their rum and lost most of his spare change to them. Eventually the two men fell asleep, but Paul was too disturbed by the clanking of serious machinery, the bloody tang of rust, and so opened the book he had taken from Mam's. He had started reading it at Gaetan's. The damp there had swollen and buckled its pages and there were translucent spots where drops of his sweat had fallen. Paul liked the idea of the book breathing in the air around it. He was not really reading it – he had trouble with the antique French and the pious tone. He was looking at the engravings instead, remembering how Genie used to make up stories around them. But some of the pages were missing. The book was falling apart.

They docked at Port Mathurin late the next morning. Paul did not walk around the centre but instead headed straight to the terminus, where he took the first bus that came. His intention was to ride to the end of the line. The bus was heading towards the southwest of the island, which Paul was hoping would be wilder and less inhabited.

Rodrigues was like rural Greece but with a slightly fantastic feel, he thought, as they drove towards the centre of the island, through a landscape more dramatically moutainous than Mauritius. Like Greece but in the time of Legends, when the world was new – it was in the mineral glitter of the light, the grass so lush it looked wet and everywhere, *cabri* – small mountain goats – feeding on terraces fenced in by black rock. But, where the cyclone had passed, the earth

162

had turned to mud and flowers broken off from bushes were strewn about like litter. Men were working hard to rebuild the place; Paul saw the sweat glittering on their skin, their muscles rippling like wind on water and all of them shouting out to one another, the inevitable chaos that came whenever desperate people tried to restore order. If you kept rebuilding parts of the island laid to waste after each cyclone, he thought, eventually the original Rodrigues would disappear altogether.

His thoughts wheeled along steadily at the same pace as the bus, but then it swerved suddenly and the brakes screeched and Paul was jolted – a dog had run out into the road. It looked back at him, affronted, and continued to jog along, its colouring that of an overripe banana, its tail the shape of one too. The fruit on the trees and the dogs in the street – that was what he'd loved best about Mauritius, Paul thought. Rodrigues was just like Mauritius used to be, the men on the boat had told him sadly. Before Mauritius got corrupted. And what about them? Paul thought. Were those men corrupt? Were they going to corrupt Rodrigues?

Somewhere outside the village of La Ferme the bus got a flat. Paul broke off from the other passengers, who were strangely uncomplaining, and walked towards the village, where he stopped at the nearest house, a square cement block painted pink. A middle-aged woman in a housecoat answered the door, which opened directly onto the front room. Behind her, two young boys in Liverpool strips lay on the sofa, watching cartoons in the way children did, deep in concentration, unsmiling.

Do you know of any rooms to rent around here? Just for a few nights?

Are you a tourist?

I suppose so, Paul replied. I'm just travelling around.

The woman shrugged. You could stay here.

Marie was a prostitute, Paul soon realised. Her customers dropped in at all times of the day and disappeared into a back room with her. They would stop off on their way out to pat the boys on the head or fix something which Marie pointed out – a leaky tap, a wobbling chair. At no point did she proposition Paul. He was half offended, half relieved. She later told him that the two boys, who never seemed to wear anything but their Liverpool strips, were her grandsons. Their mother was in Mauritius, working in a hotel. He'd been given her room.

He did not feel comfortable here, in some strange woman's room. Her dressing table was crowded with personal things. He thought of Mam's at 40 St George's Avenue. He thought of the woman at Sainte Croix, and her little shrine of cosmetics and plastic religious statuary. The window was so high here that his room seemed almost windowless, like a cell, and it was lit by fluorescent strip-lighting which buzzed like a bluebottle even after it had been switched off. Whenever he turned the light on, the little lizards which constantly scaled the walls froze – as though immobility somehow rendered them invisible – then scattered in a second. Everywhere you stepped there were insects, but you only caught a glimpse from the corner of your eye before they slithered or scuttled away. Their constant presence put Paul on edge – he did not like the unexpectedness of insects – but the lizards he liked. Their eyes shone with a beady, benign intelligence. And they ate mosquitoes.

One evening, as Paul lay in his room trying to read, he heard the boys come in late from playing outside. He heard Marie slapping their backsides, demanding to know where they'd been. Tearfully, they told her about an abandoned shack they had found, whereupon more bottom-slapping was heard, Marie punctuating each slap with strict orders not to explore

164

such places – had they not stopped to consider why it had been abandoned? There could be scorpions in there, she said, or ghosts. The boys howled with retrospective terror.

The next afternoon, when Marie was busy with a client, Paul found the two boys in the yard. He asked for directions to the shack. They had lied to their grandmother about how far into the wilderness they had strayed. The shack lay somewhere between Pointe Pistache and Baie du Nord. Paul headed north and then west of La Ferme, for the coast, as directed, then walked southwest along the beach, heading down the coast. He came to a stretch of shoreline where the grass bordering it was silvered with salt, and fell upon a shallow river that didn't quite meet the sea. Perhaps it had run out of energy, although when the rains were up perhaps it swelled and flowed out into the sea and perhaps there was a point then at which the fresh water and the sea water mingled. Paul had heard that sharks liked to gather where rivers fed into the sea, because fish were plentiful there.

He walked until eventually he spotted a spit of land, where perched at its tip he could see a small bamboo shack, overlooking rocks and the open sea, exactly as the boys had described. It had a straw portal and a zinc roof. A piece of zinc pulled across the entrance served as a door. Paul peered around it. There was no one inside. He looked back at the beach. It was deserted. He pulled aside the zinc and went in. He found only a pile of old blankets. What would it be like to live there? he wondered. How lonely would it feel? The surrounding grass was littered with smashed-up bits of shell – the land must recently have been underwater, probably during the cyclone. The shack must have been built after that. He wondered who had built it and if they still lived there. Years ago in Mauritius, on a trip down to Le Morne to see Gaetan, he and the gang had passed an abandoned cabin. Paul had wanted to go inside but Jean-Marie would not let him: just setting foot in the place would send you mad, he'd said, there were so many bad spirits inside. When Paul had asked for the story Gaetan couldn't tell him anything. Only that runaway slaves had sheltered there; that something terrible had happened.

Every morning for the next few days, Paul walked to the shack to check that it was still abandoned. When, after a week, he found that the place was still empty, he decided to move in. On his way back to Marie's to collect his things, he wondered if there was a myth about that place, as there had been with the shack in Le Morne. He decided he didn't care. He was not superstitious.

But, that night, he dreamt about the shack.

(xiii) The Story of the Shack

A man lived in a shack by the sea. This man had been a slave, but had been freed. Feeling himself disgusted by the human race – by the capacity for man to enslave man, for the enslaved man to turn on his equally unfortunate brother – the former slave decided that true freedom lay in a world where he could live alone. So he did not follow his newly freed brothers and sisters who formed communities, nor did he follow those who had ambitions to travel beyond the island of their enslavement, freedom for them being the opportunity to see new worlds. Instead, when the day of his liberation came, he walked for two days in the opposite direction from everyone else, away from all signs of human habitation, to the other side of the island. The wilder side. No one wanted to live here, where the sea was too rough to bathe or swim in. But the insolent power of the sea here pleased the man, since the boom of the waves on the shore sounded like cannons, warning off others. The brutality of life on the wild side did not scare him. As a former slave, he was inured to hardship. So he camped in a forest by the sea, and there, over many days and nights, the man set about clearing a plot of land where eventually, over the course of many more days and nights, he built a shack. Having made a home for himself, he tilled the land around it. He kept no animals: he could not bring himself to fence in any living thing. He spent his days tending to the garden, or fishing in the river. He would take walks in the forest and examine any new plants he found for signs of possible use, or of beauty. His nights were spent by the fire, singing songs he half remembered, or staring into the flames where strange visions appeared to those who dared look long enough. The man lived in peace like this for many months. But one day, when he awoke, the man felt uneasy for the first time since he had been set free. The shack was filled with a strange sort of light and an unnatural silence. At first, he thought an angel had come to him. He had heard that angels emitted a terrible light and that their presence stilled the very air and, with it, all sound. But no angel appeared. Setting off into the forest to investigate further, he noticed that the wind had assumed a higher pitch, like the whine of an injured animal. This was all that could be heard. The man felt that creatures who normally inhabited the forest with their myriad sounds were all watching him silently from their hiding places. And when he reached the beach he saw that a malevolent yellow light had descended on the world like a fever and that the waves were as tall as trees. On seeing this, the man understood and was filled with a sense of great joy and exhilaration. He had lived through many cyclones during his time on the island, but he had never before witnessed one. The master had always hidden his slaves in the basement of the big house whenever a cyclone was predicted, for fear of losing them. So to witness a cyclone – indeed, to have his house – his home, his labour of many months – destroyed by one, and perhaps even to *die* in a cyclone – why, now he was truly free!

A plane in the sky: a trail of white for a wake – the world had turned upside down and for a second the sky became sea, and the plane, a faraway boat.

London, Mam said.

What's London? Paul asked.

Where that plane is probably going.

This was Paul's first ever memory. He was three years old. He and Mam were with her new husband Serge. He had taken them to the beach. It was Serge who had pointed out the aeroplane.

Paul did not like the beach, which was never as nice as it looked from a distance. The sand was soft, but littered with pieces of bleached coral, hard as bone, some shaped liked the skulls of small mammals. And half buried in the sand were sharp bits of shell, smashed up by the sea, and the spiny needles and tiny cone-like seeds shed by the filao trees which bordered the beach. They hurt his feet. Paul preferred the garden at Serge's house, where they now lived. He liked to rub his hands on the squat palms, whose trunks felt as though they had been knitted from some thick yarn. He liked the citrus colours of the hibiscus flowers, the steaming early morning grass. But what Paul liked best about the garden was the fruit on the trees. Lemons or mangoes or lychees. It was like something out of a cartoon, something magical. And then it turned into a kind of mania for him, so that every time he passed a tree or a bush he would peer into its foliage, try to look beyond the shadows and the leaves to see what fruits were hanging there. He was always convinced there *would* be fruit, though he was too small to reach, so he would ask Jean-Marie to help. Jean-Marie was Serge's son. His sort-of brother. But Jean-Marie was older than Paul. Almost a man. Jean-Marie would part the leaves for him and pick whatever he found. Jean-Marie would cut them open just in case – thrillingly – there were *bebete*, or insects inside, holding out a slice on the blade of his pocket-knife. Sometimes the fruit was surprisingly sweet or creamy-tasting, sometimes musty and complicated. Sometimes, there was no fruit at all.

Jean-Marie, like Serge, was dark, blue-black dark like a prune. His hair stood out from his head in wild curls. The whole of him was a gravitational force. He made the world spin for Paul, the way he picked him up and swung him around, hoisting Paul onto his shoulders or tipping him upside down until he was screaming and red-faced, with excitement or fear he didn't know, until Jean-Marie set him upright, the world still turning and churning with the pull of water being sucked down a plughole.

Paul spent a lot of time in the garden, playing alone. And then, one day, he was called into the house. Mam was cradling a baby. Its tiny fingers waggled randomly like the antennae of an insect.

Bebete, Paul said.

Serge laughed. No. Virginie. Like the girl in the story. *Paul et Virginie.*

Genie, said Paul.

Life changed when Genie was born. Now that she was in the world, Paul felt strangely more alone in it. Before, he had had no sense of himself as being separate from the universe. Playing in the garden, he had felt no difference between himself and, say, one of the trees. But with Genie's existence Paul had acquired a small, persistent shadow. It was your shadow that gave you a sense of the limits of your body. It was Genie that made him Paul.

Other things changed when Genie came. Mam was unhappier. Angrier. The first time Paul noticed this was the day he found a snake in the garden. He ran screaming into the house. But when Serge came out to see for himself, he whisked Paul up and swung him around and laughed because it was not a snake, it was a *kulev*, which meant good luck. He was going to the races that day. So he took Paul with him, heaving him up onto his shoulders so he could see the horses better. Paul screamed and screamed for their horses to win but none of them did. After the races were over, everyone drifted away and Paul helped Serge to pick through all the discarded betting slips which littered the ground, looking for winners that might have been dropped by mistake. Paul was doing important work here and he confided this to Serge. Genie would have been no help to them and Serge agreed.

Yes, he said. This is men's work. This is no place for a little girl.

When they came home, Mam seemed to know as soon as they walked in that Serge hadn't won. She said in a sharp voice that the *kulev* was not lucky after all and Serge tried to laugh and said, Why, maybe it was. Maybe he would have lost more if Paul hadn't seen the *kulev*. But Mam didn't laugh. She said, Gambling is the opposite of work, and Serge swore and threw some coins at her. Paul rushed to pick them up, anxiously, not wanting things to be all over the place like that, worried that Genie – asleep in her basket in the corner – might wake up.

But sometimes, Serge won. Then he would buy things. One time he bought chickens, and a cockerel, Milord, which would wake them with his crowing. Milord was fiercely territorial. Whenever Paul was out in the garden and passed Milord's patch of yard the cockerel would run for them (Genie, now walking, followed Paul everywhere), his sharp beak pecking at the air, hoping to strike. Once he caught Paul. Serge dismissed the injury, saying that Paul should leave the poor bird alone. Paul got angry then, and later that night he had a nightmare about Milord. As he thrashed and screamed, Mam came rushing to the bed and shook him out of it. He and Genie now slept in a bed together in a curtained-off area of the front room, and the next day when Genie woke up her face was covered in bruises. Paul was shocked and ashamed that he had hurt his sister. It's all Milord's fault, he muttered, but Serge did not agree and punished Paul.

Jean-Marie did not intervene, but later that day, when they went out into the yard, Milord was gone. For dinner that night they ate *kari kok*. Paul refused to eat it. That meant Genie refused to eat her food too. So Serge sent Genie down from the table. Then he tipped her food onto Paul's plate, telling him he would stay there until it was cleared. Mam got angry then and had a row with Serge which only ended when Paul bent his head to his plate, gagging slightly as he ate, the tears rolling fast, plopping from his chin into his food.

Jean-Marie was not there that evening. He was like a dog that could feel a cyclone coming. He had a talent for disappearing at times like these. You only knew he was gone when you heard the sound of his motorcycle starting up, then it faded away, and that always sounded sad to Paul, like someone saying goodbye. Sometimes Paul would run down the road after him.

Whenever Mam and Serge fought, Paul would run out into the garden. There was a hole in the garden wall. He put his eye to it. He saw the street dogs and the street children; he saw goats being herded past. He saw Jean-Marie's friend, Maja. Maja came towards the wall, unzipping his pants, and poked his *gogot* through it.

Touch it! he ordered.

Paul put his finger out and touched him. Then Maja laughed and ran away.

And once Paul saw a funeral procession, the mourners in black, wailing, eyes rolled into their heads.

When Paul was older, he would stay out in the street long after his schoolfriends had gone home. Or he would go down to the garage where Jean-Marie worked, and if Bossman wasn't around Paul would hang out there. On such occasions, Jean-Marie let Paul help him when he worked on his motorcycle, teaching him the names of all the parts and tools. Paul loved the way Jean-Marie spoke to him when they were working together, asking him to pass this or that in a businesslike manner, like an adult, an equal – as though he really was of use. Not like Maja, who always treated Paul as though he was in the way, and gave him a nasty nickname, *Caca Tibaba* – Little Baby Shit.

Sometimes Jean-Marie would bring Genie to work with him too. He would capitulate to her demands to be hoisted onto his shoulders – normal walking was far too pedestrian for little Genie – and she would sway happily there as he led the way down the alley to the garage, an infant empress in her palanquin, Jean-Marie as solid as an elephant as she slapped her fat little hands against his head with excitement.

Eventually the fighting got so bad at home that Jean-Marie left. He went to live in a room above the garage where he worked. One day, Paul came back from school to find that Jean-Marie's bed had gone from the lean-to. Paul regretted bitterly that he had not at least been asked to help with the move, but Jean-Marie laughed.

I have hardly anything to move, he said.

Then he told Paul that next time Bossman wasn't around he should come to the garage and check out his new pad. And that was what Paul did after Mam and Serge had had their last ever fight.

Mme Blondel next door had given Genie a bag of Neapolitans – little buttery cakes, covered with pink icing and sandwiched together with jam, made for weddings or christenings. When Genie took the bag home and showed Mam, Mam got angry and took it from her. Mam didn't like the neighbours, she said. They didn't like her. And then, when Serge came home and Genie told him that Mam had taken her cakes, Serge got angry. He slapped Mam and left the house, slamming the door in an echo of that slap and leaving Mam to slide down the wall, the way shadows did, weeping bitterly, the cakes rolling about her on the floor.

We are going to London, she told Paul and Genie, as they gathered up the cakes. Just the three of us.

London, Paul said to himself, and the name tasted of cold metal.

He slipped out of the house and made his way to the garage. The doors were open and Jean-Marie was on his back, working on a taxi-cab. There was no sign of Bossman.

Jean-Marie, have you ever been to London? Paul asked.

Wait a minute, said Jean-Marie, getting to his feet and rubbing his greasy hands on his overalls. London?

Paul repeated what had happened earlier, and what Mam had told them. Jean-Marie was quiet. No, Little Brother, he said. I have never been to London.

Has Serge ever been to London?

No, said Jean-Marie. Serge has never been to London.

Do you know anyone who has ever been to London? Paul asked.

Jean-Marie looked at him for a moment, as if deciding whether or not to tell him a secret.

Yes, he said finally, I do know someone who has been to London. In fact, I know someone who is *in* London *right now*.

Who? said Paul, and Jean-Marie said, My girlfriend.

Paul did not know that Jean-Marie had a girlfriend. But yes, he did, and she lived in London. Jean-Marie had kept her a secret from them all.

Come, he told Paul. Let me show you.

He climbed the ladder which led from the garage up to his room under the eaves, and Paul scrambled up after him. It was a slant-ceilinged room accessed via a hatch in the floor, and it was covered in posters of girls in bikinis, and motorbikes and bare-chested Kung Fu fighters. Paul was filled instantly with admiration and envy. In the corner was Jean-Marie's camp bed, covered in a bedspread Paul recognised from home, the one with a yellow and green and brown diamond pattern which made Genie think of snakes.

Jean-Marie sat down on the bed and reached under it, pulling out an old cigar box. He opened it and took out a cassette tape. The track listings were handwritten in purple ink, in English.

This is from my girlfriend, Jean-Marie said. She gave it to me before she went back to London.

Then he took from the box a photo, which he handed to Paul. It was of a girl – a *blonde* girl – in a bright blue bikini. Jean-Marie told him the photo had been taken at Grand Baie, where she had been on holiday with her family. Jean-Marie had met her at a disco there. Paul stared at the photo while Jean-Marie told him about the girl, whose name was Annabel, and all that she had told him about London: the trains which ran underground, the lady prime minister with her handbag, and people called punks, like Annabel's brother, who had dyed his hair green and pushed a safety pin through his nose and spat on people at parties.

Jean-Marie played the tape and told Paul about his plan to go over to London and see Annabel again. The tape finished playing and Jean-Marie put it on again.

If you are in London, I will come and see you too, he said.

By the time Jean-Marie had sent him home for dinner, Paul could sing along with the chorus to 'London Calling'.

In London, Mam insisted they spoke only English. So they wouldn't get confused, she said. Paul soon forgot his Creole. But, for a long time after that, he still dreamt in it.

PAUL
and
GENIE

(i) Genie

...Rodrigues.

Does he know *whereabouts*? How *wa*s Paul? Did Gaetan say?

I told you, Mam – he didn't say much at all. All he said is that Paul left for Rodrigues over a week ago.

What language were you speaking in?

Creole. Well, sort of. I know all the words, I can hear them in my head but I have to think really carefully before I open my mouth. Like people who have to point to the words when they read.

So – are you going, then? To Rodrigues?

Yes. I've come all this way. I go the day after tomorrow. Tomorrow Gaetan is going to show me around the island. He's borrowed a car.

Ah. I wonder if it will come back to you at all?

What?

Mauritius. Your memories of it.

I keep telling you, Mam. There's *nothing*.

Genie returned to the day room where Grandmère was watching the soap she liked to follow. Mam's phone call had annoyed her, specifically her questions about Mauritius, about Genie's experience of being 'back', as she called it. Why not come out herself if she was so curious to know what it felt like to be here?

And how *did* Genie feel? She couldn't tell yet. She'd only just arrived. There had certainly been no shock of recognition

on her journey from the airport the day before. There was...
nothing. The same blankness Grandmère experienced when
faced with Genie herself, it seemed. Oddly enough, Mam
seemed more interested in Genie's having forgotten Mauritius
than she was in Grandmère's not remembering Genie: surely
that was the tragedy here? But Genie was grateful that,
stranger though she was to Grandmère, she did not seem to
mind Genie taking her hand. The heliotrope cologne with
its smell of Madeira cake that Genie had loved so much as a
child now made her quite helpless with nostalgia, as they sat
together watching *Secrets de la famille*.

She was amazed that Grandmère could follow its
convoluted plot when just that morning she had greeted
herself in the mirror as her own dead sister while Genie was
helping to do her hair. Every character in the soap seemed to
present a different story to everyone they encountered, so
corrupt were they.

That man, Genie asked, nodding at the television. Who
is he again?

He is the secret bastard brother of that woman who is
in love with him, said Grandmère with a confidence that
suddenly aroused suspicion in Genie. It occurred to her then
that Grandmère probably had no idea who these people
were and that she most likely made up new identities and
associations for them each time she watched.

When the programme ended, a nurse Genie had not yet
met came in to call them to dinner. Her tightly curled hair
was so uniform in appearance, Genie wondered if it was a
wig. Genie introduced herself and explained that she had
come to stay for a couple of days, that her mother in London
had arranged it.

Well now, said the nurse. She gets no visitors for years
and then you and your brother come to see her one after the
other.

It was as though Genie had just glimpsed Paul from the corner of her eye.

The home where Grandmère lived was in Vacoas. It rained a lot there and the building – this guest room – smelt permanently of damp. Genie's skin too was permanently damp. In fact she found it hard to tell where her skin ended and the damp air around her began. She kicked off the sheets and lay naked, looking up at a reproduction of an antique map of Mauritius – Isle de France as it was then. It did not show where she was now. Genie had no interest in seeing the island. She was going on the trip tomorrow out of politeness to Gaetan, who seemed so keen to please her.

When she'd asked Grandmère to tell her more about Paul's visit, what she'd got instead was an account of another time Paul had been to see her: years ago in London, when he'd asked for the money which he'd used to run away. Genie had realised that it was not so much that Grandmère did not remember her – more that she did not seem to *see* Genie. In her company, Genie felt spooked, but, oddly, she herself was the ghost – Grandmère talked in the present tense of a Genie from the past. And she had done the same when she talked of Paul.

Had Grandmère, so absent from the present, re-enacted that same meeting with Paul when he'd come here almost four weeks ago? Would he not have felt haunted then himself by the ghost of his younger self? And how deflating, that *déjà vu*, when he was reminded he had once again – at twice the age he'd been the first time round – run away to Mauritius.

If anything, it was not recognition or connection with the island that Genie felt, but alienation – it was odd to hear the language of home and family in the mouths of strangers. But perhaps, Genie thought, drifting to sleep in this small whitewashed room that made her think of a nun's cell, it wasn't quite true to say she remembered *nothing* about the island. Hadn't she had a strong sense of *déjà vu* herself earlier that day? When she'd got off the bus at La Gaulette and walked to Gaetan's village – a place she'd never been to before – it had all been exactly as she'd imagined it: the cement-shop with the faded Pepsi mural, the tamarind tree and the old guys drinking under it. That was to say, it was all exactly as Paul had described it to her.

Dimun isi sovaz. The people here are savages.

She was not sure if Gaetan meant 'savages' or 'wild', or if this word had a slightly different meaning in Creole.

I don't need a bodyguard. I was born here.

Gaetan shrugged and got back into the car. He had wanted to bring Genie to the house where Jean-Marie and her father had lived, forgetting, if he'd ever known, that Genie had spent the first five years of her life there. The road was called Sparrow Street. All the streets had English names. She couldn't remember ever having known this address, though perhaps she had done, once. Of course the house was much smaller and poorer-looking than she'd remembered, one storey high, its blistered yellow paint revealing patches of cement underneath. The wrought ironwork over the windows was almost ornamental, but there was no disguising its function, Genie felt. She couldn't see the hole in the wall that Paul used to look through, the one she could never reach herself. But she could see over the wall now. She recognised some of the trees in the garden, and the bush in the corner where Paul had once seen a snake.

The car was old, and had no air-conditioning. They drove with the windows down, Genie carefully shifting in her seat every now and then to detach her bare legs from the hot, sticky plastic.

Where are we going now? she asked.

To see your dad and Jean-Marie.

Genie realised without shock that she had no idea where they were buried. 'In Mauritius' had always felt like enough of an answer. As though the island itself were a cemetery.

I'd rather go to the beach, she said.

Gaetan thought she was joking. And, clearly, that the joke was in poor taste. Genie tried to explain.

You know how, she said, if you dream, and you dream you are back at school, say, only it looks like your grandparents' house, but it's *not* your grandparents' house, it's your school, and how you know it's your school even though it doesn't look anything like your school but it's your school because it *feels* like your school?

Your Creole's not bad, Gaetan said.

I can't instantly picture my dad or Jean-Marie but I recognise them in dreams. I know when I am in their presence, I know what it *feels* like to be around them. I know when I'm dreaming about them, even if they're not there. But if I see those slabs of marble, I will never have that feeling again.

I'll take you to Flic-en-Flac, said Gaetan. Where the Mauritians go.

The car park smelt of diesel and frying spices from the fast-food vans. It smelt of pineapple too: a man sat peeling and chopping piles of the small local variety, Victoria, the syrupy smell mixing with curry and sea salt on the breeze, the sound of the waves overlaid with the knife's *hack-hacking*. Gaetan stopped to buy a few slices, which he shared with Genie. They ate greedily, the fruit intensely sticky and sweet. While they ate, they noticed the pineapple man's small daughter. She was dressed, quite bizarrely for a day's work at the beach, in a pink satin frock that looked like a bridesmaid's

183

dress. It was slightly too big for her. When a friend of the pineapple seller's then turned up with a tired-looking horse, its eyelashes thick with flies, they watched as the little girl accepted a ride. She was lifted, unsmiling, up into the saddle, wearing a solemn, almost regal expression as the horse plodded on, neck drooping, in a circuit of the car park.

She looks like a little doll, Gaetan said. Gaetan himself looked like an antique grizzled teddy bear, Genie suddenly thought. They walked through the trees, towards the beach. Mauritius seen from the plane had made Genie laugh. It had seemed ridiculous, too like images from the in-flight magazine. But close up, down here, on the west side of the island at least, it was not really like that. The sky was quite full of clouds and not at all the breezy blue you saw in postcards. The sun glared. It was very different from the more touristy beaches in the north. Gaetan was right: this was a beach for Mauritians.

I like it here, said Genie.

Me too. But some people don't appreciate it. They'd rather live in a place with twenty million people and more shops and bigger cars and an underground railway system and big giant advertising screens flashing everywhere you look. Not me.

They went and sat in the shade at the edge of the beach, near bougainvillaea bushes covered in flowers of every kind of lipstick colour. They were surrounded by families, here for picnics, with their tupperware containers full of curry and their jumbo bottles of pop and towels and even tarpaulins which they had brought from home and stretched out between the filao trees so that the babies and old people could sit in the shade. They had made themselves a home from home. Every now and then one of the older folk, left out of the conversation, would look over at Genie, as though they knew her.

And Genie was beginning to feel she knew them. The landscape had triggered no memories except those implanted by Paul – descriptions of his own memories. But hearing strangers speak Creole no longer made the language strange to her. Instead, it somehow made the speaker more familiar.

You'll like Rodrigues, Gaetan said. It's quiet. Small. Like a village. It's like Mauritius was fifty years ago. That's what everyone says.

Wouldn't you like to live there?

No. You can't go back in time like that.

Genie was watching a family of four wading in the shallows. The mother was white and looked English, the father Mauritian. But it was the two children who caught her attention: a boy of about eight and his much younger sister, both honey-coloured like Paul, with the same blonde-brown hair that had the singed look, Genie always thought, of old flower petals. And on the breeze she caught high-pitched squeals in London accents.

Do you think I'll find him? she asked, lying back on the sand.

I don't think he wants to be found. But I don't know if you are willing to give him that choice.

Genie closed her eyes and wondered why voices on the beach always sounded so far away.

(ii) Paul

He did not sleep well on his first night in the shack, unused to the sound of the sea and the cold from the wind which crept through the cracks. He mummified himself in the blankets the previous occupant had left and sniffed the rough wool pressed to his face. Strange to know them as a smell in the dark. He slept only when dawn broke, daylight somehow calming the sea.

When he awoke, he stood looking out at the edge of the spit, towards the horizon. *Not quite on land and not quite at sea.* There were times in London when he would get claustrophobic in places where he couldn't see the entrance or exit, but here he felt free. You could see the entrance or exit – the sea – from everywhere here, on what he was beginning to think of as an island, his island, on the island of Rodrigues. *This haunted rock.*

(iii) Genie

There were many myths about lost treasure buried on this island, the taxi driver told her. Genie looked out onto the ochre and black landscape, the tough grass, the stones of lava strewn about as though spelling out a message from a lost time. It was wild-looking here, the grass overgrown, broken trees which had not been broken cleanly; the splintering made her wince. The island was still in tatters after Cyclone Kalunde and it made sense, she saw now, that Paul had run here to hide, a broken man among the broken trees. She tried to read in the stones, in the curve of a slope, in the twist of a wind-stunted tree, some sign of Paul.

(iv) Paul

Paul walked up the beach and into the trees, collecting branches that had been torn away in the cyclone. Later, he would make a fire. In between the broken trees others stood whole: palm trees that had yellowed in the heat, a baobab trailing desiccated entrails like streamers. *Man, your family tree, it's like a baobab.* Maja had said this, when Jean-Marie had introduced Paul to the others as the brother of his sister. The coconut trees looked faded, tired; they leant towards the ground, heads bent with fatigue. It was the sun. The sun was so hot, even the sea was barely able to lift its head, it seemed.

Reaching a stream, Paul drank from it, splashing water on his face and chest, the ripples of light on clear water like the stretch marks on Eloise's breasts. She'd got very thin very quickly. He would wash that blanket, he decided, and he returned to the shack. As he pulled aside the zinc covering the entrance, he was reminded of all the times he and Sol had done just that – pulled away boards or unscrewed sheets of Cytex to discover, like hermit crabs, empty shells where they could make a home. Paul had believed then that he and Sol were equal in terms of ambition and prospects. They hung around together, did drugs, rescued broken things from skips, destroyed them in creative ways, living only in the present. But Paul realised now that he and Sol had never really been the same at all. Sol always busy in a way that Paul could never be: he himself was energetic, yes, but nervous and edgy and ultimately directionless, as though, quite literally, he'd never known what to do with himself.

Long after they'd fallen out (Eloise had 'let slip' exactly what had happened the night of Genie's fifteenth), he would hear about Sol – going straight edge, or giving up squatting for renting – and had gradually come to realise over the past year that the lack of any kind of progress in his own life at this age was actually a kind of regression.

Let me make this a home, he thought, momentarily forgetting the blanket, opening up his suitcase to find that old book and pull out a couple of pictures from the loose binding. A pubescent Virginie, bathing in a secret glade, one hand held to her breasts in a provocative gesture of modesty, some kind of ancient muscle memory of those experimental twelve-year-old's wanks tugging at Paul. And '*Paul sur le rocher*', the boy now a man, sitting hunched on a spiteful-looking rock, looking out to an empty horizon. These he propped up against his suitcase by way of making the squatted shack a little more his. Then he turned to the mattress and pulled the blanket from it. As he did so, a yellowed newspaper cutting fluttered out. He read it. Then he folded it carefully and put it in his pocket.

Later, in his search for food, Paul walked along the Baie du Nord. There he came across a snack shack by the side of the road. A boy of about twelve stood behind the counter, reading a book. He was wearing glasses with thick lenses and frames so large they looked as though they'd been stolen from some old man. Paul was surprised by his sudden urge to laugh. When had he last found anything funny? A radio on the counter was playing a *seggae* and the boy was nodding his head in time to it. Paul had heard the song a lot in Mauritius: 'Peros Vert'.

Hello.

Paul realised this was the first word he'd spoken aloud since leaving Marie's place.

What are you after? the boy asked.

A glass case on the counter held dhal pancakes, and slices of aubergine deep-fried in batter. Tins of soft drink were displayed in pyramids behind him on a shelf.

I'll take a can of Pepsi. And some of those aubergines.

As the boy filled a paper bag, which immediately broke out in greasy patches, Paul asked, That little shack out on the rocks, on the way to Pointe Pistache... He described its exact location.

Yes, I know it.

Who lives there? Paul asked.

The boy shrugged. Nobody, he said, handing Paul the bag.

Any idea how long it's been there? Who built it?

Ti Jean. After the cyclone.

Where is he now?

Dunno, the boy said. Nobody does. His house got smashed up in the cyclone. He went a bit strange after that. Said he didn't want to rebuild his house. So he built himself that place on the beach. And then he got worse. Started ranting about God punishing us for our sins. That was why the cyclone came, apparently. To punish us. Then he just disappeared. Maybe he got washed away with his sins.

Paul laughed.

Are you a tourist? the boy asked.

Not really.

The boy asked where Paul was from and Paul said, London. The boy asked lots of questions about London, which he'd never visited, never having left Rodrigues. Then Paul asked about the book the boy was reading. It was called *Benares*.

Benares is a place in India, said the boy, But it's also the name of a place in Mauritius. This is about the Mauritian Benares. It's funny, don't you think, to have two towns in different countries with the same name? I would like to visit Benares in Mauritius and then Benares in India. And also London. You know there is an East London in England but did you know there is an East London in South Africa? That's where my grandfather came from.

What's your name? Paul asked.

Jeannot, said the boy.

Gaetan had liked that song a lot – 'Peros Vert'. And on Paul's first night there, when he'd been drunk and they'd been talking about Jean-Marie, it had even made him cry. He liked the words, he'd said to Paul helplessly, wiping away the tears – a lament for the island which the singer's family had been forced to leave. That was what they called the island: *Peros Vert*. Green Peros. Did Paul know that was in the same group of islands Maja's family had come from? It made him wonder, Gaetan said, how Maja would have turned out if he'd had the opportunity to live his whole life on the island where he'd been born. Paul thought of Maja as he was now. Had he come full circle, somehow? Become the person he should always have been? If so, he'd had to kill someone to do it.

Paul carried the branches he'd gathered down to the shack, where he set about building a fire. Crouching by the pile of branches and dried grass, ready to set it alight with matches, he heard Eloise: *Like rubbing two damp sticks together*. She had said that about failing to orgasm on whatever medication she'd been on at the time. He remembered their goodbye hug. He had held her very tightly and for a long time, until she'd pulled away oh, so gradually, pressing her forehead gently into his chest and levering herself up and off, as though she were unpeeling herself from him. So that was it now. She had changed, and he had not.

Over the last couple of years it had seemed to Paul that a succession of possibilities had one by one become closed to him. A life with Eloise was just one of these. Paul thought then about Jeannot and his plans to visit parallel places and smiled. As he sat staring into the lazy flames, shifting every few seconds to present a different part of his body to the heat now that the sun had suddenly sunk out of sight in a brief blaze, he realised that it did not disturb him to think of his life in this way. Left with fewer options, it was easier to make decisions. He supposed all his remaining options would gradually fall away until he was left with only one: the only decision really worth considering.

(v) Genie

It had been apparent to everyone Genie had met back in Mauritius that she was a foreigner, even before she'd opened her mouth. She'd wondered if it was her clothes, her haircut or the particular quality of her brownness, which glowed in a fresh way (she liked to think, looking closely at her new colour whenever she stepped, dripping, out of the shower), built up from a greyish London base coat with successive layers of tan. When, in Mauritius, people had identified her as foreign, they had commented. And, when they commented and she replied, they heard the accent and seized on it, happy to talk to someone from London, happy to have been proved right.

But not this man. This Rodriguan. This man with the high, narrow shoulders that brought to mind Paul's had no interest in her at all. And why should he? To him she was just another Western tourist.

She was sitting at the hotel bar drinking coffee, making a plan. She'd hoped to engage the barman in conversation – wore an expression which conveyed this, she thought – but after serving her he'd turned back to his task of chopping up fruit for the evening cocktails. His manner changed when he was joined by a colleague – a pretty girl with eyelashes so thick they looked frilly. The two flirted as they manoeuvred their way around each other in the cramped space behind the bar, so cramped that the waitress knocked over a glass of orangeade and swore, apologising briefly in French to Genie.

That's OK, Genie replied in Creole. The waitress looked up at her suspiciously, gave a brief, tight smile, took up her tray and sashayed out towards the pool, asking the barman, over her shoulder, to clear up for her. His name was Regis, Genie noted.

Was it very bad here after the cyclone? Genie asked, again in Creole.

Yes. They're still clearing up now. There are still food shortages. But not here.

Was he trying to reassure her, or was he being sardonic? She hoped not. She felt that his sarcasm – if sarcasm it was – was being used against her, was meant to further the distance between them. More so for being in Creole, which Genie had chosen to converse in for the opposite reason. She guessed that must be his intention: after all, he had not commented on the fact that she had spoken to him in his own language, when she was clearly – with that accent – a foreigner. This man couldn't care less. His indifference, coupled with the shy dimples that had emerged only in the presence of the waitress and disappeared when she left, annoyed Genie intensely. Suddenly she snapped, I'm not here on holiday you know.

Oh?

I'm looking for my brother. She took out the photo of Paul. Have you seen this guy around?

No.

He's definitely here.

Plenty of places to hide in Rodrigues, he said. If you don't want to be found.

I suppose.

Genie wanted to say, Your island is not as big as you think it is. It's tiny. I'll find him.

But you know, he said, looking straight at her for the first time, everyone on this island has to go to Port Mathurin at some point. And if not your brother, then someone who has seen him, at least.

The bus to Port Mathurin was old and blew out emissions so thick that Genie thought instantly of some hooved animal, stamping up clouds of dust. After she had paid the conductor, a middle-aged woman with rust-coloured hair and rust-coloured eyebrows drawn in with pencil, Genie showed her the photo. She told the conductor about her search for Paul but the conductor said nothing. She had that lost look that tourists always wore when listening to directions you and they both knew they would forget as soon as you walked away. After that, the woman's gaze turned to rest on Genie, that same look, whenever she was not otherwise occupied with the other passengers – schoolchildren in dazzling white uniforms, scrawny old men in short sleeves and straw hats. You never know, Genie said to herself. The people you see around you. They could all be lost to someone.

Not much of a capital, Genie thought, walking the dirt-packed road that led to the centre, though like any tourist she was delighted by the little painted shacks and the women in woven hats selling lemon pickle and bottles of tiny red chillies. She remembered what Gaetan had said about the island: that it was like Mauritius from an earlier time, nothing more than a village, really.

Gaetan had taken her lack of interest in Mauritius personally, she saw now. But once he had given her all the useful information he had to offer – that Paul was now in Rodrigues, having gone over by ship over a week before – Genie had seen no reason to stay on. Grandmère had no idea who she was. And why wallow in sentiment when she felt nothing about the place? That, to her, would have been dishonest. And anyway, it was not the past that interested her, it was the present, and Paul's absence from it. That was what she was here for.

Compared to Rodrigues, Mauritius was like London. She had not recognised any of it from her childhood. She had thought then that countries were not home – families were. How could she feel at home in herself with Paul missing?

But, over the course of the afternoon she spent wandering around Port Mathurin, something here struck Genie deeply. It was the slowness of the place, the unguarded manner of the people, the underdeveloped look of it. Rodrigues seemed more foreign to Genie, more far away from London, but it seemed more familiar too: more like how she'd imagined the Mauritius of her childhood to have been. The actual Mauritius she had just left seemed almost as brusque, as wary, as littered and light-polluted and full of noise and agitation as London in comparison. No wonder she hadn't recognised it as part of her *past*.

The centre of Port Mathurin was a few narrow streets laid out in a grid and lined mostly with those painted zinc shacks, low cement buildings and larger, more ornate colonial buildings which were governmental residences or offices. These last were set back from the road behind high walls. Over one wall hung the branches of a frangipani tree. Genie caught a whiff of its scent, so strong it was almost obscene. She disliked the flowers, which were too ripe, too fleshy: they would not fade and die quietly like English flowers, but looked as though they'd go straight from full bloom to rot.

Why are you trying to find him? Gaetan had asked, as he was driving her back to the home in Vacoas.

Because he's lost.

(vi) Paul

If Ti Jean was still alive, he might return at some point. He would want his shack back. Paul was squatting the place, after all. But, listening to that wind last night and the waves which seemed to be creeping ever closer, Paul guessed that it might be the island itself which evicted him. This was what he thought, standing on the edge of his rock. This was what he did now, every morning when he awoke. Pulling aside the sheet of zinc which had sung all night in the wind, he would look up at the sky. He would walk out as far as he could on the land until it turned into rock and stand looking out to sea. This morning, something about the light brought back his dream, the one he'd had almost every night since *that* night. And now he remembered it: him and Genie in Mauritius, taking a trip down to Gris Gris on Jean-Marie's motorbike. When they'd run out of road, they had left the bike and continued on foot over huge silvery rocks that looked like wads of chewed-up chewing gum (she'd said). Feeling his way back into the memory of the dream and its almost pleasurable sadness, he remembered that nothing much happened. Nobody died. It was just unbearably, beautifully sad. They were climbing over these rocks, him and Genie, down to an amazing stretch of sea, when Genie had stopped to inspect some plants at her feet. She'd asked him what they were. Dunno, he'd said, pinching off a leaf to sniff. Pine! he'd said. They're little pines. Must be the coastal wind. Stunts 'em. Weird, he'd said, I've never seen tiny little pines like these before – and then he'd noticed her giving

197

him this strange look – this very sad look – and he'd said, *The blue honey of the Mediterranean.* That's what Fitzgerald said.

Honey. *Just like honey.* Eloise, stroking his skin, would sing that to him sometimes. On his way to the snack shack, the song played in his head. He had been to the shack several times now. He liked to listen to the boy's radio, liked the way the boy was always dancing around, even while seated, and he liked hearing him talk about books. The boy was crazy for them.

Today, when he saw Paul approaching, he smiled.

I've got a surprise for you!

Don't tell me Ti Jean's turned up?

This was a running joke of theirs. Jeannot laughed and brought out a flask from under the counter. Soup!

Soup? For me?

Lentil soup. You eat the same thing every day. I thought you might like a change. It's what we had for dinner last night.

That's great. Thank you. I'll give you the flask back tomorrow.

You can give it to my mum.

Your mum?

I'm not going to be here from now on. I'm going back to school tomorrow. I told my mum about you. She asked all sorts of questions. She asked me what you were doing here. I didn't know what to say. What *are* you doing here?

When Paul returned to the shack he looked through his things. He wanted to find something to give Jeannot. But, looking through his suitcase, he found nothing of worth. He had only basics with him – 'prison possessions' he called them. Genie had always hated that joke. And the pills, he had those too. An old book that was falling to pieces. And a silly story besides. He could find nothing to give the boy. He was angry and confused by his sudden urge to cry.

Later that afternoon, he walked back to the snack shack. He had with him the flask, which he'd washed out in the stream. And the newspaper clipping he had found under the mattress. He thought the boy might find it interesting.

The story concerned a man from – oddly enough – a small village near Benares, in India. This man had suffered with stomach pains all his life. He was too poor to see a doctor. But finally, when he reached his thirties, his stomach had distended to the point where the pain was unbearable. He sought treatment. Cancer was suspected but the results of blood tests proved inconclusive. Finally an X-ray was performed. It was discovered that the cause of the man's pain was his unborn twin, who had fused with him in the womb and had been growing inside him all these years. An operation to remove the twin revealed that he had adult-sized hands, feet and genitals. His head was covered in thick hair. He had teeth.

Asked how he felt about the situation, the man said, I am shocked. I have five sisters. I always wanted a brother and he was growing inside me all my life. And now he has been taken out of me I have no pain. But I feel as though I have killed him.

(vii) Genie

Today the *Mauritius Pride* had arrived. Genie stood for a long while on the docks, staring down into the milky green water, breathing in the hot smell of sweat on skin, dead fish, rubbish, salt and rust, wet rope and seawater, watching the flow of people and goods on and off the ship. Boxes of hi-tech hardware and sacks full of rice and sugar, and a Jeep. Wicker cages full of chickens, strings of dried octopus. Genie stood mesmerised by all this activity until it began to slow down. Then she approached a man who seemed to have some official status in connection with the ship. He wore only a pair of orange surf shorts which looked almost fluorescent against his black skin. She tried to get his attention but he did not seem to hear her, instead turning to signal someone, raising his arms and pointing to confirm his instructions.

Genie tapped him on the arm and felt a slick of sweat. He turned to her, tossing his head coquettishly, a gesture which set his finely plaited hair swinging and one which he carried off quite elegantly, Genie thought, for such a fat man. He made an impatient gesture. Genie realised then that he was deaf.

She asked as clearly as she could, in French, if he worked there. He looked closely at her mouth but did not seem able to follow her words. After her third attempt at explaining, the man grabbed a colleague and signed to him. This man turned to Genie and asked what the problem was.

Do either of you work here? she asked.

Yes, we both do. On the *Pride*.

Genie showed them Paul's photo and asked if they'd seen him. The interpreter shook his head, but his colleague nodded and began to sign. He was on the crossing, two weeks ago, said the interpreter, following his friend's gestures. He sat on deck with a couple of guys – other passengers – for almost the whole journey.

Do you know where he is? Did you get what he was saying to those men? Do you know who they are? She turned from one to the other as the interpreter repeated these questions to his colleague, each followed by a businesslike shake of the head.

He says all he can tell you is that the guys he saw your brother with seemed like bandits if you ask him.

Genie thanked them and gave them her details. As she turned to go, she stopped in her tracks and called out directly to the man who had seen Paul, forgetting for a moment that he could not hear her: why had he noticed Paul? How was it he remembered seeing him? It was two weeks, after all, since Paul had travelled over.

This time the interpreter quoted his friend directly.

He looked foreign. But not like any tourist or even a businessman. I wondered what the hell this guy was doing over here. There is nothing for him here.

It was half-past four in the afternoon by the time she made her way back to the bus stop. She had been waiting for twenty minutes before a young boy in school uniform walked past and asked her what she was waiting for. A bus, she told him curtly, as though he had been sarcastic. But they stop running at four, he said. Then, with the air of someone used to being disbelieved, he sighed and asked a couple of passing schoolgirls what time the buses stopped. Each girl looked at the other, fingers buried deep in a shared bag of sweets, as though it was a trick question.

Four, they said, almost in unison, barely able to talk around the bulges in their cheeks. The boy looked at Genie as though to say, You see! and walked off without a word.

It did not take long after that for night to fall, for the darkness to deepen and the barking of dogs to sound louder, now that the roads were quiet. Walking back through town in search of a taxi, Genie's heart lurched with the approach of each shadowy figure she passed. It was at times like this that she forgot about Paul completely, thought only of the moment, of immediate dangers – though later it occurred to her that if Paul was in Port Mathurin he might only show himself when the streets were dark and empty, and that perhaps one of those figures she had shrunk from had in fact been him.

(viii) Paul

This morning, the sky was pale and complicated with cloud which was the grey of something that had once been white. In the distance the sea, out on the reef, was a tingling blue, the foam so bright, it made the clouds look even dingier. What a triumph of Earth over Heaven, Paul thought, there on his rock, remembering the story Eloise had told him, the one *he* had once told her, apparently. He was living like a monk. He drank water from the river that failed to meet the sea. He ate food that he bought from the shack: fried fish or dhal pancakes. He wondered what the boy had told his mother: she'd seemed tense, had avoided his gaze. He would buy his food and drink from her and she would push his change towards him on the counter without looking at him. On his last trip there the woman's eyes had glittered in a funny way, as though she was about to spit on him. He did not feel like going back there again. Besides, this food did not agree with him. His digestion had deteriorated. His gut would go slack and he'd get the runs or else it would knot him up with constipation. One day when he was squatting under a hibiscus bush, straining, he looked up to see two small fair children – he couldn't tell if they were boys or girls, they were that young – staring at him. He scrambled into the bush as their mother appeared to retrieve them. He heard her scold them in some Scandinavian language. Tourists. He saw a few tourists from time to time on the beach. They arrived in monstrous vehicles which rolled heavily over the landscape. But soon it would be winter and, sweet and mild though it was, the tourists would leave. They were like the drunks who visited curry houses back in England and only wanted it hotter than they could stand it.

There might have been tourists around, but Paul was alone. And why would you say this except to mitigate the meaning of those words? You could not say them to anyone else, or at least, not to anyone you would expect to understand. If you could, the words would no longer be true. You said them to yourself, in your head, and you heard them echo. You heard the echo and you thought, I am alone.

Paul thought, how could anyone be alone with so much life around? So much insect life? If that was not a contradiction in terms.

There were ants in his shack. The cockroach he had heard clatter across the packed earth of the shack's floor in the night lay dead on its back by morning, the ants feasting on it.

He remembered a cockroach he'd waged war on at Marie's place, shortly before moving to the shack. He had seen it two days running, in the shower hut. It sat in the corner with its face (did they have faces?) towards the wall. On the third day, Paul had had enough of it. He took the shower head, switched the water on and aimed the jet of water at the cockroach. His intention was to swill it down the drain. When it began to drift on the water in semi-circles, like a leaf in a storm drain, it panicked, feelers plastered against its head like two wet hairs, scrabbling away from the jet of water, which Paul continued to train on it.

Paul had looked at this cockroach and its frantic efforts and felt almost a respect for it, or for life, or for its instinctive urge to live. But also disgust: why should it want to live so much? Why should the instinct to live be more developed in a cockroach than a human? The simpler the creature, it seemed, the more urgent its instinct to life. After all, didn't pandas and lions in the zoo lose the will to live sometimes? And didn't people? Paul could never imagine a cockroach pining away with loneliness.

Eventually he had given up on the cockroach, feeling sorry that he had started this, feeling pity for it or respect or annoyance because it was taking so long to die. The minute he switched off the water, the cockroach made a run up the wall and slid off, onto its back, where it shuddered and twitched with a violence that led Paul to think it was finally dying. He let it be and left. When he returned the next morning it had regained consciousness and was upright again in the corner, staring at the wall.

He would walk to Port Mathurin later. Stock up on food there. Get drunk.

Out in the street the sky glared like brushed steel. But he could barely see in here. The girls lounging in the doorway of the rum shop had hung back to let him pass into the single dark room. The one window high up in the roof was small and covered in chicken wire, like the door of a rabbit-hutch. He thought back to that night in Sainte Croix and the stacks of rabbit hutches out in the yard. There was nothing but a few rough tables and chairs here, and a poster advertising Guinness. Paul sat down and ordered rum from a boy with a pencil behind his ear. He looked at the girls in the doorway. One of them was quite young, younger than Genie. She was tall and dark with a great cloud of frizzy hair and large, shining eyes and her white dress looked whiter in the gloom of the place and against her skin. She smiled at Paul encouragingly but he turned away. He sipped at his rum, but when he next looked around for her she was sitting at a table in the corner with a man Paul recognised as one of the sailors from the ship. The sailor looked at him and said something to the girl, laughing. He did not have the dreamy look of the fishermen Paul knew in Mauritius.

Paul ordered another rum from the boy, who after serving him returned to a chessboard he'd set up on the bar. The boy was apparently playing against himself. Paul thought of Eloise – of a visit he'd made to her in some private institution shortly after they'd split up. She had always worn her hair long and wild, stroking at it absently as though pacifying a cat that was trying to get her attention. So when she'd walked into the visitors' room it had been a shock to see that her hair had been hacked off.

I get it, Paul had said lightly, realising with a lurch that she'd cut it herself. Self-harming. Is that what you're in for this time?

I like it like this. Makes me look thinner.

Oh, disorderly eating again.

There had not been much else to talk about then, in that plain room with the high windows, until a pale girl with lilac-coloured skin had come in, followed by two people who were probably her parents. I played chess with her once, Eloise had said, nodding at her. She plays like a fucking kamikaze.

Paul tossed back the rest of the rum, then signalled to the boy that he'd take another. Until that conversation, he'd never even known Eloise could play chess.

Several rums later, the sailor left, and the girl in the white dress came to talk to Paul. She wanted to know who he was. What he was doing here. Where he was staying. Her questions annoyed him. I am going to tell you one thing about myself, he said. I am going to tell you about my sister.

When he had finished talking, she put her hand over his. He pushed it away, stood up. Staggered out into the metallic light. He stood in the doorway of the rum shop to steady himself. He did not know how long he had been standing there before he heard someone shouting his name.

A London voice.

He looked up sharply. There she was, at the end of the street. *Genie*. She was running towards him. *At* him.

He ran.

(ix) Genie

Genie wandered back up along the street, ignoring the stares of everyone who'd seen her run screaming after him – the shopkeepers in their doorways, the people at the roadside stalls who had paused, snacks held halfway to their mouths, to watch the chase. She had lost him by the port. Now she was on her way back to the rum shop she'd seen him leave, to ask about him.

A couple of girls were sitting at the rough wooden counter that passed for a bar.

A man came in here, Genie said, laying the photo down in front of them. I need to know where he is.

The two girls looked at one another and laughed.

He's my brother, Genie said. Our mum is sick. I need to find him.

They gave her their full attention then. One of them, the younger one, a tall, goofy-looking girl in a grubby white dress, spoke. I tried to talk to him, but he wasn't very friendly. I asked where he was staying and he wouldn't say. I wanted to know what he was doing in Rodrigues and he wouldn't tell me. But he did tell me about his sister, she said.

I'm his sister.

Not you. The sister who died.

What are you talking about?

His twin. The tumour. In his stomach. The one he has lived with all these years. He told us he had had this terrible pain all his life and then when he went to the doctors they told him he had a cancer but when they did some investigations on him they realised it was not a cancer but it was his twin sister. She had got stuck to him in the womb and had been growing inside him all this time. He had to have her cut out, he said. He was here to recover. He said he was full of guilt because he felt like he'd killed her. Is that true?

Without replying, Genie turned and left.

(x) Paul

This morning it was diarrhoea. He squatted, felt his gut go slack, pulled some leaves from the hibiscus bush and wiped himself, shaking a little and suddenly weak. He'd go for a bathe in the sea.

He looked up at the sky. It was hard to tell what time of day it was. Today, the sky was white, harshly lit. It looked like a London sky before snowfall. He had not seen snow in a long, long time, he suddenly realised. For a second he wondered if he ever would again, and then he caught himself: was that it? Had he unconsciously made the decision never to go back to London?

He recalled the first time he had ever seen snow: the memory of Genie's encounter with it was more vivid than his own. She was five. She had stood in the middle of the garden in her red galoshes, with her mouth open, uncertain whether to laugh or cry. And Paul had shown her there was nothing to be afraid of, even though he could not be sure of this himself. He pointed out, when it settled, its static, fibrous quality, like magnetised iron filings, the way it crackled on the skin and felt rough on the tongue. Soft as fur, but ruffled, like the hackles on the back of a cat's neck. Paul had felt bad for Genie when it all melted days later and the stuff turned to a dirty red brown slush and they saw what it had been covering – all the rubbish and the shit – all the rubbish and shit in the garden of 40 St George's Avenue, the garden Genie had always hated. He remembered how she had hated its long damp grass which hid, she was convinced, all manner of repulsive creatures, such as the snails that were clustered at the edge of the path. Paul would walk along it and jump with both feet onto any snails he saw, taking great delight in the crunching sound, while Genie picked her way through them as though they were mines. If ever she trod on one she would leap up howling as though the soles of her feet had been burnt. Paul found this funny. One afternoon, he had guided her towards a robin he said he could see in the bushes.

Where? she'd asked, looking up, stepping ahead, as Paul had planned. Kerrrrunch.

But before she could scream, the sky had ripped open and it had started to rain – fat drops that fell heavily like a shower of stones. In a second they were soaked. She and Paul had looked at each other, laughing with the shock of it.

Come on! he'd said, taking her hand and pulling her back towards the house. He grabbed the hem of Genie's anorak, and pulled it over their heads. Icy drops slid from the plastic onto their foreheads, stung numb with the cold, and as they ran up the path he looked to see Mam at her rain-streaked window looking out at them. When they got inside she was waiting at the door with rough towels. She'd wrapped Genie up in one and rubbed her hard, while Paul shook himself like a dog.

Well! Mam had said. Like Leda's children, in the same shell.

Paul got to his feet, dizzy, shaking, and made his way back to the shack.

(xi) Genie

When the sun went down, the floodlights round the hotel pool went up, and a sudden golden-blue glow filtered through the curtains of Genie's room. Out by the terrace bar a *sega* band was setting up, and the sound of instruments being tuned broke through Genie's sleep. She had passed out earlier that afternoon. She lay on her bed, staring at the veins of light on her ceiling, reflections from the pool.

She got up and wandered back out to the bar. Regis was still on duty. He did not look up at her as she took a stool at the bar but continued making up a cocktail, which he then pushed in front of her.

On the house. You might need that.

The bar was still empty. Most of the guests were getting ready for dinner.

Was I really drunk?

Really drunk. You should go out there and listen to the band. He smiled. Tourists love that shit!

How many times? I'm not a tourist.

You *might* have mentioned it earlier. A few times.

Tourism. It's a form of prostitution. That's what my brother said when he came back from Mauritius. It's true. You let these rich people in, they give you money, you treat them like gods.

You don't tip like a rich person.

The waitress came back to the bar with her empty tray. While Regis was making up her order he asked what *she* thought about tourism as prostitution.

Her name was Katy. She looked Genie up and down. Oh, well, me, I see tourists more like *children*, she said. When a tourist dies here or in Mauritius, it's big news. The way it is when a child dies. Drownings mostly, but every now and then something worse. Something one of the locals has done. I always feel like the death of a tourist is worth more than the death of one of us.

That's true, Regis mused. Whenever a tourist dies there's this feeling that all of us are responsible somehow.

We were responsible for looking after this person and we failed, said Katy. She flashed a smile at Genie, collected the beers and went to deliver them.

Genie looked closely at Regis. The dimples had gone.

What are you doing here? she asked. In Rodrigues? Why haven't you left?

Why should I? It's my home. Where my family live. My sister. I've seen enough of the outside world – the people that come here, what I see on the news – to know I don't need to see any more of it. Maybe that's how your brother feels. Maybe he's had enough of it.

He doesn't even know how he feels.

And how, *mademoiselle*, do you know that? *You* don't know what he feels.

I know he ran away from me yesterday.

So you kept saying earlier. And he wouldn't have done that if you hadn't gone looking for him. I tried to tell you that the first time I met you, when you came here showing me his photo. As though you were a *gard*, or he was a lost dog! Maybe he just wants to be a tourist for a bit. I don't mean stay in a swanky hotel. I mean, have a holiday from his own life. Leave him to it. If he wants to come back, he will.

But he never will, she thought suddenly.

Rodrigues was the sister island of Mauritius and Paul, she thought, was her brother island, remote and totally isolated but somehow connected and, as Rodrigues was to Mauritius, a dependency. She realised now that she had thought this all her life: she was supposedly the baby sister, the younger one, the less clever one even. But she knew, and Paul did too, that she was the stronger one. Was this because she was younger? Paul had been alone for the first five years of his life. Her arrival must have changed his world. Genie had never known such a disruption, would never know the solitude he'd experienced before she was born. And then Genie realised – and the thought made her gasp almost – that for her it would be the opposite. She would know it if Paul were to die before her. She thought about what Gaetan had said. About how Paul would not want to be found, but how Genie was not giving him that choice.

She drained her cocktail. The *sega* band had started playing and guests were starting to wander out of their rooms to the poolside. The sound of clinking glasses and laughter floated over to Genie as she walked past the pool and into her room. She went over to the desk, switched on the lamp, sat down in front of the pad of hotel letterheaded paper, and picked up the pen beside it.

Let him have his choice.

(xii) Paul

Something was squatting on his chest. Or that was how it felt, anyway, when his struggle for breath shook him. Something was squatting on his chest, breathing in his face.

Oh God.

He felt the panic start to form over him like skin on boiling milk. He didn't know what to do when it got him here, right here in bed, in the only place he felt he could escape it. There was nowhere left to go. He had to fight his way out of it. He had to think of something so that he didn't start thinking too hard about breathing and thinking that if he stopped thinking about breathing he would stop breathing for good, and when he got to the point where he thought he was about to stop breathing he started scrabbling at the dark with his fingers, as though trying to slit his way through it, as though he were in mourning and rending his clothes.

He lay on the mattress, squinting at a black stain on the floor. It appeared to be dissolving, then intensifying. The ants. They were moving in the purposeful way of commuters. They could have been people observed from a satellite. He lay there for some time watching it spread and contract, pulse of its own accord. This unnameable pain which he still carried – the name of it always on the tip of his tongue – had long since broken up and the bits floated free around his body now like clots. He watched the stain dissolving. He stared at the ants, trying to distract himself from the sound of the sea, from the fact that he remembered too much. He remembered the time he had brought Mam the daffodils. He'd looked out into the weed-choked beds of the gardens and seen them, almost hidden by the overgrown hedge. So bright they were! So yellow against the dark wet green! And he'd run out and tugged them all up, and made a great glorious pile of them which he'd gathered, running back into the flat, into Mam's room and she'd slapped him round the head, for pulling them all up, for dropping them on the floor, for running into her room without knocking where he had surprised her, standing naked, looking at herself in the mirror.

There were the memories. There were the ants. And then, Paul thought dully, there were the pills. He leant over to his suitcase and pulled it open, reaching for his washbag. He pulled out the tub of pills and twisted it open. Then he shook out one of the pills, and swallowed it.

(xiii) Genie

Genie lay by the pool in her bikini, blindly groping from time to time for the cocktail set down next to her lounger. She felt the sun trail red shadows across her closed lids, and was gradually succumbing to the rum that thickened and slurred her thoughts. Tomorrow she would leave. She would fly back to Mauritius, and, from there, home to London.

Her Mauritius, she realised, was imaginary, cobbled together from a few patchy memories and the stories she'd heard from Paul and from Mam. But Genie was more Mauritian than Paul, technically (this was only ever half the story, Mauritius, half his story, and funny how the white half was the dark half, she thought). You could also argue that Paul was more Mauritian than her: he'd spent more time there. And, unlike him, Genie had never felt the desire to return. Perhaps she was afraid it would disappoint her. Or perhaps she saw Mauritius as more his than hers. It was like childhood, she thought, looking at a little girl playing in the pool. You can't ever go back. Every morning this little girl waved to Genie, and Genie always offered her a small smile in return. She knew the little girl read it as sad, lonely. But in fact she was simply tired: tired out by the heat, the salt air, the silence, the long hours spent alone, the effort not to think of Paul, the rainbow of cocktails she worked her way through each afternoon by the pool. She had written Paul a letter and left it with the girl in the rum shack. He would know where to find her if he wanted to see her. But she would no longer be looking for him.

She took another sip of her drink. It was layered, red and yellow. She took her swizzle stick and swirled it around. Mauritian could just be another word for 'mixed'. Their mixes were just different, that was all. Everyone was a bastard there, on that bastard island – the bastard of England and France left to grow up wild in the tropics.

She heard squeals and splashing and opened one eye to see the little girl paddling erratically towards a beach-ball her father had thrown into the pool. And now, having reached the ball, she was shrieking with delight and frustration, struggling to cling to it in the water.

The further away you were from a past hurt, Genie thought, a self who got hurt in the past, the more you felt as though that self wasn't you. It was more like your child, an innocent whom you, as an adult, with your advanced perspective, your advantage of hindsight, should be in a position to protect.

Genie had become more and more angry with Paul. So what? What could she do about it now? All she knew now was, how could he? How could he do that to her? How could he leave her like that? Like this? She and Mam always used to say to Paul, You think too much. Now Genie would have added to that – of yourself.

Mademoiselle? There were dimples now whenever Regis said this to her in public. She looked up into his face and thought groggily, Dark skin kind of concentrates you, makes you occupy a more sharply delineated space. If you were white here, in this blinding light, you'd kind of melt into the whiteness of the sand or the sky.

He handed her a piece of paper. She sat up, unfolded it. It was a hand-drawn map. She looked at him, puzzled.

My sister has a small snack place near Baie du Nord, he said. Your brother's been seen there a few times. He's living nearby, on the beach.

(xiv) Paul

Look at me, bringing poison into Paradise! Paul thought, reaching for another pill. There was a time when he'd debased his coinage: he cut his drugs, crushed them to dust, sold them as space dust. Dust from space was radioactive. And people who took this stuff glowed in the dark. They emitted heat. There was an expression in Creole, *pa koze*: don't talk. It implied absolute agreement with what someone had just said: I know what you mean. No need to explain.

The first time he and Sol had taken an E together – Paul's first ever time – out in that field, the grass brushing his ankles like Eloise's hair on his bare skin, the sky frosted with stars, they had looked at one other and said nothing. And then he in turn had introduced El to Es in another wordless but eloquent encounter. To think they had ever called that stuff Ecstasy, he laughed. How naive they'd been. These days it was more Mild Excitability. Not even that, he thought, thinking about the increasingly frequent waves of paranoia that licked the edges of his consciousness whenever he took pills in London. There had once been an innocence about it (or had it been about them?) that had been cut with something cruder, over the years. When had that happened exactly?

Now, as he took another, he didn't talk. But the sea would not shut up. The sound of it was beginning to engulf him. It was ceaseless. For variety he imagined that the noise outside was rain. Rain or the constant sound of cars on a distant motorway. It could have been the wind in the coconut trees, the flapping of ragged banana leaves or the faint roaring sound when he put a shell to his ear or when he couldn't sleep at night. Like tonight. Like every night. Anything but the sea.

There was a bush by his shack. Paul had no idea what it was, but the needles were spiny, as spiteful-looking as the black railings he used to see everywhere in London. When it rained heavily, the sound of the drops on its whip-like branches was like a large animal drinking, lapping something up, or like the sound of fire. And the wind sometimes sounded as if it was drumming at his door (the piece of zinc he had to drag open or closed), demanding to be let in. But he swallowed it. Paul realised that, when it came down to hardships you couldn't change, mistakes you couldn't undo, you just had to swallow them.

(xv) Genie

She had taken him for a tree at first – one which might have escaped the cyclone, it was so slight. And then, as she walked further along the beach, she saw it was a man, and then she saw in this figure a much thinner, darker version of Paul, his profile smudged by the grown-out hair, the beard. He was standing on a ledge of land which stuck out over the sea, just looking out, as though scanning the horizon for a ship, as though watching the sun set, but now all that could be seen of it was a bar of hot light at the horizon, and the sky, fast deepening.

Paul!

Running as she was screaming, hoarsely, out of breath, over the sand which was packed hard and cold where the sea had rolled over it, her bare feet slapping flat on it, flip-flops in hand, like running on rain-wettened London pavements. He did not turn around immediately, as though the sound of her cry took a long while to reach him.

Paul!

He saw her and moved slowly down towards the beach where she was running to meet him. Without a word he stepped forward, and when she folded him into her arms she was shocked to discover how little of him there was left.

(xvi) Paul

He dreamt she'd come to see him. He'd been standing on his rock, watching the setting sun bloody the sea, and he'd turned to see her on the beach, approaching him. He could see her mouth open, knowing that she was calling to him, but could hear nothing for a while, and then he'd heard his name. It had seemed ages since he'd heard his own name from someone else's lips.

And when she'd thrown her arms around him she had felt more solid than she'd ever felt in real life. She was sobbing, and when finally she'd stopped crying she'd asked him to go back with her. Told him it would be better for him that way, that if he was sorry about what he'd done to her, if he wanted things to change, then this was his chance. He could not remember much of what he'd said in turn, only that he could not go back, and then she'd looked at him, quite closely, and asked what was wrong. And, when she asked, he couldn't tell her. That was the ultimate wrong, that he should have to say what was wrong with him. Come with me, she'd said. And he'd said, *The blue honey of the Mediteranean*, that's what Fitzgerald said.

And she'd looked at him as though finally she understood, and then she had started crying again.

There were more and more tourists around. Paul saw them walking along the beach and they looked up and saw him, with his beard, standing against the lilac sky, under the roiling, boiling, biblical clouds. They never approached. Paul

222

shook his fist and thought, What a triumph of Heaven over Earth! The sky was electric! All glare and clouds; the sky frowned with clouds.

He felt like one of the desert fathers. The desert fathers were not fathers, they were as barren as the desert itself. Oh, yes, in another life, they might have had children, wives, livestock, unpaid taxes, unsupportable debts... but here, in the desert, they were free.

He couldn't be sure but he thought he'd been here for some time now. It could have been weeks. Perhaps months. Had he come here to lose himself or to find something? God, perhaps? If so, Paul had not found him. Not in the empty, endless sky, the stony, sparsely seeded ground that stretched red and cracked as a washerwoman's hands. It was not as lonely as you'd think, he thought, the desert. So far he had encountered other men, hermits like himself, stripped to the waist, their scrubby beards hanging down their chests. They did not acknowledge him as they passed, respectful of his solitude; they scuttled across his horizon, anxious not to disturb his view or block his light. But he wanted to stop them as they passed, wanted to stay them with his scrawny grip, tight as an old man's or a newborn's or a madman's, and tell them, Don't go. The devil appeared to him at noon, shimmering in the heat haze, his eyes the size and colour of gooseberries. The world was a desert full of men wanting to be alone.

Here in the desert, water was scarce so he didn't wash. And washing off this red dirt which had settled on his skin like brick dust after a demolition would distance him from his environment, his purpose: would make him less of an element of his surroundings and more like an intruder. His own smell made him feel less alone. His body was a forest of smells. But the memories: these made him feel more

223

alone. When a man was shipwrecked, even in the desert, all his memories returned to him. His memory became as pin-sharp as the desert island sun and nothing escaped its glare.

And it was like that when you drowned, of course – your life flashed before your eyes. Once was enough! you thought, as you lived through it all again, drowning in memory, a wine-dark sea, and they crowded in on you, breathlessly, the memories – once was enough! But then, wading into the black sea, wading into the night, gasping with cold, watching the dust melt away and your skin come up glittery with salt, slippery as a newborn's – as you waded out to the point where your feet floated free and you lost touch with the earth, like walking on water, like dreams of flying, as you gradually found yourself out of your depth and the water closed over your head, stinging your eyes, like crying in reverse, and you started to swallow your tears, the thoughts burst like bubbles in your mouth and filled your lungs and it all flashed before you – once was enough – but then you were glad to know at last, after a whole life of searching, the moment when everything had gone wrong.

Acknowledgements

This book would not have been written without the love and support of my first and best reader, Luke Williams. He's the greatest friend known to woman, man or dog.

Thank you also to Candida Lacey, Corinne Pearlman and the team at Myriad, particularly Vicky Blunden, for her sensitive and intelligent editing, and Linda McQueen for her heroic copy-editing.

Thank you to Cathryn Summerhayes, for her unfailing enthusiasm, warmth, good humour and tenacity.

Thanks to Andrew Cowan for the encouragement and brilliant editorial advice.

Thank you to those who read the book closely and offered much support during its writing: Rattawut Lapcharoensap, Richard Misek, Chris Power, Stan Roche, Natalie Soobramanien, Hilery Williams, Caroline Woodley.

Thank you to Amit Chaudhuri, Maureen Freely, Ali Smith and Christos Tsiolkas for generous encouragement.

Thank you to Barlen Pyamootoo for the conversations.

My family have been great. I owe thanks to Arlette Ta-Min for taking the time to read the book and comment on it, and to Harry and Mona Ramasawmy for their hospitality, and for showing me around Mauritius. While there I also stayed with Gaby and Doris, who spoilt me rotten, and got to know my cousins Shane and Rudi and Kevin and Kenny, who showed me the island. Thanks to you all, and also to Armio and Jacqueline.

Thanks to Gom for taking me to Rodrigues, and to Sarojini Ramasawmy for accompanying us. And thanks to Mum and Dad for the writer's retreat in Brittany.

Two of the stories in the book were written while on a residency at Cove Park. Thank you to Polly Clark and Julian Forrester for inviting me there.

Thank you to everyone who read the book or chapters of it in its early stages: Eleanor Birne, Jon Cook, Sara De Bondt, Oliver Emanuel, Jon Evans, Sara Heitlinger, David Lambert, Robert McGill, Belinda Moore, Andrew Motion, Tiffany Murray, Sarah Ridgard, Iain Robinson, Kathryn Simmonds, Peter Straus, John Thieme, Simon Trewin, Zoe Waldie, Yair Wallach, Jason Warren, Saul Williams and Jo Wroe.

And finally, thank you to my dearest Rob, for all the love and support, for the beautiful first edition of *Paul et Virginie*, and for crying at the end.

Author's Note

There is currently no standard orthography for Mauritian Creole. I have based mine on Baker and Hookoomsing's *Dictionary of Mauritian Creole* (L'Harmattan, 1987) and the version of Ledikasyon pu Travayer's *Prototype Mauritian Creole-English Dictionary* that is available online at www.lalitmauritius.org.

Genie's immediate impressions of Rodrigues are based on my own translation of an extract from Jean-Marie Le Clézio's *Voyage à Rodrigues* (Gallimard, 1999). Gaetan's story about the island of Saint Brandon is a retelling of one in Le Clézio's *The Prospector* (David Godine, 2008).

Another version of Grandmère's story about the lost dog first appeared in Luke Williams' *The Echo Chamber* (Hamish Hamilton, 2011). Further information about *Genie and Paul* and Bernardin de Saint-Pierre's *Paul et Virginie* are available at www.genieandpaul.com.

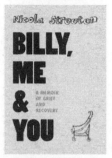

www.myriadeditions.com